T. S. YAVIN

KAR-BEN
PUBLISHING

For Pearl Davidowitz Fisher,
who taught me, nurtured me, cheered for me, loved me,
and always did like All-Star season

Kar-Ben Publishing, Inc.
A division of Lerner Publishing Group
241 First Avenue North
Minneapolis, MN 55401 U.S.A.

Website address: www.karben.com

Library of Congress Cataloging-in-Publication Data

Yavin, T. S. (Tovah S.)
   All-Star season / by T. S. Yavin ; illustrations by Craig Orback.
      p. cm.
   Summary: After competing both in the Jewish school they attend and on the baseball field, ninth-grader Reuven and his younger brother Avi find that teamwork is better than competition.
      ISBN-13: 978–1–58013–211–4 (lib. bdg. : alk. paper)
      ISBN-10: 1–58013–211–1 (lib. bdg. : alk. paper)
      [1. Baseball—Fiction. 2. Jews—Fiction. 3. Brothers--Fiction.] I. Orback, Craig, ill. II. Title.
PZ7.Y279Al 2007
[Fic]—dc22   2005035988

   Manufactured in Canada
1 2 3 4 5 6 – BP – 12 11 10 09 08 07

1

Reuven stomped across the infield, kicking gritty clouds of dust out of his way. He stomped past the puddle-pocked pitcher's mound and past the bases marked with moldy slabs of cardboard.

Reuven didn't see any of that. Not today. Today, Reuven didn't see this quiet neighborhood park that he and Avi and Dad used for Sunday morning practices.

Today, Reuven saw that other baseball diamond, on the other side of town. The one with the perfectly groomed mound and the freshly painted white lines marking the base paths. Today, he smelled that newly mowed grass, and he heard his name echoing down from the loud-speaker system.

And now . . . the starting pitcher for tonight's All-Star game . . . Reuven Silver!

Reuven couldn't help himself. He drew in a deep, sweet

breath and smiled. What a great, fantastic, wonderful, delicious day for baseball!

"Come on, Reuven! Hurry up!"

Avi's voice pulled Reuven out of his daydream. He was glad he'd had his back turned to Avi and Dad so no one could see him smiling. Baseball was serious. Very serious. And a baseball diamond—even one like this—was a place for work, not for daydreaming and smiling.

They began long toss. Five throws. Avi to Reuven. Reuven to Avi. Then they each took two giant steps backward and started again.

Reuven couldn't remember when Dad had taught him and Avi to play long toss; it was so long ago. When they were little, it was three-way long toss. But, eventually, Dad just let the two of them play together while he coached.

"How do they know what positions we're going to play?" Avi asked as he waited for Reuven's throw.

"It doesn't work that way." Reuven flipped the ball in a perfect arc, then set himself for the return. "Spring league isn't like the teams you've played on before. They'll ask you what positions you want to play, but that doesn't mean much. In spring league, the coaches decide and you play where they tell you."

"Is everybody pretty good?"

"You remember my team last year, don't you? Everybody was good. Almost everybody."

The boys stopped to take their giant steps backward.

"You going to pitch?" Avi heaved the ball to Reuven. "I mean, do you want to pitch?"

"I might. I might try."

"Why have you been practicing so much, then, if you don't want to pitch?"

"I didn't say I didn't want to pitch. I said I might try. You have to try out." Reuven sent the ball back with a little extra spin. "You have to try out for pitcher in this league."

While the boys worked, Mr. Silver dumped their catcher's gear on home plate. Most kids didn't even own catcher's gear, but the Silvers took their baseball seriously, and Dad insisted on safety first.

"Hey, guys," he called to the boys. "Move apart some more. Think third to first. That's going to be an important throw."

They each backed up four steps this time, and after that, every throw was launched with a grunt. Avi stopped asking questions, and Reuven concentrated on the rhythm of the game.

Dad watched until they'd made about a dozen throws each, then plopped a couple of balls next to the pitcher's mound and motioned for the boys to come in.

"Registration is in an hour. Let's skip pop-ups and grounders today and do some pitching. Who's first?"

"I am." Reuven stepped up on the mound.

"Why you?" Avi grumbled. "I want to pitch first this time."

"Come on, guys. Let's not waste time today."

Avi shrugged, moved over to home plate, and slipped into the chest protector while Dad helped strap the shin guards around his legs.

Reuven's pitching form was not a thing of beauty. He knew that. He used a three-quarter sidearm motion that Dad had shown him one year when he was struggling for accuracy. His accuracy was better now, but he had never tried to change his style. It worked for him.

Reuven traded the sliding rhythm of long toss for the staccato beat of pitching. Now each throw had a big exclamation point behind it, and Reuven liked how that felt. He liked the stretched-out tug on his shoulder when he released the ball. He loved the speed of his body plunging down the sloped mound with the air struggling against his sweat-flecked face. He liked hearing the thwack of the ball as it hit Avi's glove.

"Okay, so step up your speed a little now."

Reuven stepped up his speed, and the thwacks came faster and louder. Then he got off one pitch that seemed to explode out of his hand. Those pitches always felt so good.

"EE-YOWCH!" Avi yelped, letting the ball bounce out of his catcher's mitt. He threw off his glove and took a moment to rub the deep red tint from his hand.

"Well, come on." Reuven backed up to reach for another ball.

"My turn." Avi flipped off his mask, then bent to

unstrap the shin guards.

"Not yet," Reuven insisted. "I was just getting warmed up. I haven't even worked on placing the ball, yet."

Avi groaned, put his mask back on, and crouched in position.

"We have to be fair, Reuven," Mr. Silver called.

But Reuven knew that Avi would go along, and Dad wouldn't do anything as long as Avi didn't complain about it. So he acted like he hadn't heard his father and got set for his next pitch.

"All right," Dad sighed. "Maybe, just a little more for you. I'll tell you where to put the ball. Let's work on the outside edge. Don't worry about high or low right now."

Avi put his glove in position. Reuven focused on it and threw the ball just skimming the outside edge of the plate. Avi would let him throw four or five pitches to one spot before he shifted his glove a little farther out or a little closer in. They both knew the routine so well that they hardly even needed signals.

Dad crouched behind Avi just like a real umpire and called, "Good, Reuven," when he hit the spot.

Reuven almost always hit the spot, so Dad switched to calling, "That was a little out," or "That was a little in," when Reuven occasionally missed.

At first, Reuven threw nice and easy, concentrating on where the ball went. Then he picked up speed. As the ball moved faster, the pop in Avi's glove grew louder. *Thwack. Thwack.* Reuven imagined that Avi's glove was a magnet, tugging faster and harder with every throw.

Thwack. Thwack. THWACK!

That last one was perfect. It felt great—just like he'd launched a missile. But Avi didn't seem to think it had felt so great. He bounced to his feet almost as soon as the ball hit his glove.

"That's it. MY TURN!" Avi threw off the mask, pulled off his chest protector, and bent to untie the shin guards.

"Not yet," Reuven pleaded. "I want to try one curveball."

"Nope. I don't want you to do that," Mr. Silver answered in his no-nonsense-don't-even-bother-to-argue tone. "I've told you before. You can ruin your arm forever. You're too young. Just work on speed and placement. That's all you need right now."

"But some kids threw curves last year," Reuven argued.

Avi had stripped off all of the catcher's gear and was already strolling toward the mound. Reuven knew it was too late to beg for any more pitching time. Dad had given in once, and he wouldn't do it again. Reuven sighed, then headed in.

Reuven loved baseball. He loved pitching best, of course, but playing the infield was great, too. He would imagine himself as a coiled spring, ready to pounce the moment the ball left the bat. And the outfield was fun because you got to run races with the ball.

Reuven just plain loved everything about baseball. But the one thing that he didn't love quite as much as the rest of it was catching. He could almost say that he didn't really like catching. Or even hated it.

There was so much equipment to wear. The face mask was always hot. Even the sharpest wind never quite made it through the bars of the mask to help with the sweat slithering down your face.

But Avi and Dad were waiting. Reuven put the gear on, got down in a crouch, and positioned his glove for Avi's first throw. It sailed twenty feet over Reuven's head and bounced off the backstop.

"Whoops." Avi laughed.

"Not my idea of funny," Reuven grumbled, loping back to get the ball.

"Ahh. I just wasn't ready. Watch my next one."

Reuven flipped the ball back, and the next pitch rocketed over his head, too. It took Avi ten or fifteen pitches to find the strike zone. Once he found it, he threw consistent strikes. Nice and easy, right down the middle.

"You're not throwing fast enough," Reuven called out. "Not for this league."

"He's right," Mr. Silver agreed. "You're throwing strikes and that's good. But we've got to get your speed up. Do you think you can throw a little harder?"

Reuven watched his brother work. Avi had that lanky build that made him look so much more like a pitcher than Reuven's more muscular shape. And he used a smooth overhand motion that started and stopped without an obvious beginning or end.

Reuven wished he looked more like Avi when he was pitching. Wished he had Avi's build. Still, he could throw a lot faster and a lot harder. Avi probably envied him for that. And Reuven kind of liked it that way. That's why he was a little surprised at himself when he took off for the pitcher's mound after snagging another slow, easy pitch.

"Look," he said to his brother. "You need to come farther forward with your right foot." Reuven drew a line across the pitcher's mound with his toe. "Aim for that spot. That's where you want to land."

He moved back into position, and Avi threw a few more pitches, bringing his right foot down on the place that Reuven had marked. Each pitch came with a little more zing.

"See! Told you!"

Then Avi got off a good one. One that really hustled. One that landed with a stinging *thwack*. One that might have been almost as good as one of Reuven's pitches.

Reuven dropped the ball in front of him and stretched to his feet.

"Let's go," he announced. "It's almost time."

Reuven knew they could have stayed a little longer, and he knew he'd gotten more pitching time than Avi. But that last pitch of Avi's had been a little too good. It had left Reuven's hand stinging and his stomach churning.

They gathered up the gear and made the short drive to a gymnasium a few blocks away. Tables lined one end of the room, and the front of each table had a bright red banner hanging down showing a team name. Every few minutes, a loudspeaker system buzzed and squeaked boys' names and teams' names.

Avi joined the back of the line leading up to the table marked "Tigers." Reuven hung at the back of the room, listened until the whole list had been read twice, then slipped into the line behind his brother.

"Think this is the right line?" he asked Avi.

"Sure. Tigers. That's what they said for both of us."

"I thought that, too. It's hard to hear. Maybe Dad could ask someone. . . ."

"It was Tigers. They'll tell us if we're in the wrong line."

That was exactly what Reuven didn't want. He didn't want to be in the wrong place, and he didn't want someone telling him he was doing the wrong thing, and he didn't want to be embarrassed. Reuven hated being embarrassed. He hated, even more, having a kid brother who was always so much more confident than he was—a kid brother who wasn't afraid of doing things wrong, wasn't afraid of asking for help, and never got embarrassed.

Reuven scooted in a little closer to Avi when another boy joined the line, then twisted sideways to look over the room. He spotted a table at the far end of the room that had this year's All-Star trophies, standing in neat lines. They seemed bigger than last year's trophies and shinier.

One boy was ahead of Avi, and now a couple more had joined the line behind Reuven.

"I wonder how many want to pitch," Reuven whispered close to Avi's ear.

Avi shrugged, then tapped the boy in front of him on the shoulder.

"What positions do you want to play?"

"I dunno. Some place in the infield. What about you?"

"Catcher, I guess. My brother"—Avi motioned behind him—"wants to pitch."

The boy looked over Avi's shoulder and nodded at Reuven, then stepped up to register. As soon as the boy's back was turned, Reuven leaned in close to Avi.

"Why'd you say that?" he hissed through clenched teeth.

"Why not?"

Avi twisted around to look at Reuven, pausing as his glance settled on the trophy table. Reuven shifted a little to block his view.

"Because we might both want the same thing. I mean, you just don't tell everybody. And what if I don't pitch? Or don't get picked?"

It was Avi's turn now to register, so he stepped forward without bothering to answer.

"Name?"

"Avi Silver."

"Grade?"

"Eighth."

"Uh-huh." The man at the desk skimmed down his list, then made check marks as he asked more questions. "And what positions do you want to play?"

"Catcher. Shortstop. I can pitch."

Reuven shook his head. Avi wasn't ready to pitch. How could he even dare to say that out loud? Reuven never asked to pitch last year and this year . . . well, this year he deserved it after working so hard all winter. How could Avi think he could waltz in and declare himself a pitcher? Just like that. Oh, well, his little brother would just have to figure out the hard way what it took to be great at baseball. Especially in this league.

While the man was fishing around in a box of uniforms for Avi's size, Reuven took a quick look around the room. Only a few of the boys standing in lines all around him were taller than his recently achieved five feet seven inches. Not that height was everything. Upper body strength counted for a lot, too. Most of the boys were wearing loose-fitting T-shirts, making it hard for Reuven to guess which of them, other than himself, had spent all winter lifting weights.

Finally, the man pushed a large mound of papers and a crisp, new uniform toward Avi, and it was Reuven's turn. He delivered his answers without even bothering to wait for the questions.

"Silver. Reuven. Ninth grade. Third base, mostly."

"You guys are brothers?" The man looked up and smiled. "I've got a great coach lined up for the Tigers. You'll like him. Here you go."

He shoved Reuven's pile of papers and uniform across

the table, then looked toward the next boy in line.

"I'll try pitching, too," Reuven added.

"Hmmm?" the man turned back to look at him. "Oh, sure. Pitcher. Always need another pitcher." He made another check mark on his list, as Reuven backed away.

Across the room, Avi was reaching for one of those shiny trophies. Reuven hustled over.

"What are these for?" Avi asked.

Reuven jerked at his shirtsleeve. "We've gotta go. I have homework," he announced, pulling Avi toward Dad who was waiting at the door.

"That can wait a few more minutes, can't it?" Avi insisted.

"Yeah, you would think that. But I *do* my homework. Not like you." And Reuven headed toward Dad, confident that Avi would follow.

On the way home, Avi sifted through the pile of materials—rules, practice schedules, game dates, and postseason plans.

"Hey! Did you see this?" Avi shoved one sheet toward Reuven.

But Reuven had seen it all before. He didn't need to look.

2

Reuven leaned across the kitchen table to get a better look at the papers tacked up on their bulletin board.

"Did you put this here?"

"Mmm," Avi answered without looking up from the algebra problem he was working.

Reuven frowned. Why did Avi have to do that? That bulletin board was supposed to be for school announcements and Mom's phone messages. He wished he could pull it down, but he didn't dare. If he did, Avi would demand to know why and Mom and Dad would get involved and then he'd have to explain.

So, he just pressed closer and stared at the announcement about selecting All-Stars at the end of spring season, one person from each team. It was an exact copy of the one that Reuven still had from last year, the one that had begun to tear from being unfolded and read and folded again a million times. At least the schedule for this year's games was new.

"We have a lot of Saturday games. One—two . . ." Reuven traced his finger down the row of dates and bumped against Avi's arm.

"Hey! Look what you made me do!" Avi jabbed Reuven with his elbow, then set to work erasing the jagged line that now crossed his page of work.

"Well, why didn't you do that last night?"

"Do what last night?" Dad squeezed past them both to pour himself a cup of coffee. "Avi, you're not still doing homework, are you? We need to leave."

"I'd be done by now if it wasn't for Reuven," Avi mumbled and slammed his notebook closed. "So what are we going to do about those games?"

"Miss them," Reuven said, with a shrug.

"Two games? We have to miss two games?"

"Three," Reuven corrected. "Three. The coach will understand."

"But it isn't fair!" Avi insisted. "The Christian kids get to play on their Sabbath. We're the only ones who have to miss games. And what if we want to make All-Stars? Missing games could hurt our chances. Isn't that right?"

Just then, Mom came in. She looked at the schedule along with Reuven.

"We can try to move you to another team," Mom offered.

"No, Mom!" Reuven and Avi practically shouted together.

Reuven planted his hand on Avi's shoulder. "All the teams will have pretty much the same schedule, anyway. And the man said the Tigers have a really good coach. Didn't he, Avi?"

Avi just nodded because he was munching a mouthful of dry cereal and stuffing his papers into his book bag.

"I just hate seeing you two always at a disadvantage this way. I wish there was a Jewish baseball league so you wouldn't have to miss Saturday games."

"Forget it, honey," Dad chimed in, holding his hand up to keep the boys from joining in the argument. "This is the best league around here. Very serious about baseball. Tough competition. I'm just glad we could get them in it. I know it's rough missing games, but the coach knows, and the guys will just have to do the best they can. Right?"

"Sure, Dad," Reuven answered, but he wished it could be different, this year of all years when he actually had a chance at All-Stars. He hated having to miss three of their eighteen games. Especially if he was lucky enough to get picked as a pitcher.

Reuven grabbed his book bag and his lunch bag and followed Avi and Dad out to the garage.

"You know, Avi"—Reuven slid into the backseat next to his brother—"they don't pick rookies for All-Stars."

"Really?"

"Not in this league."

"Is that a rule? I read the rules and—"

"It's not exactly a rule. But everyone knows it. I just

thought you should . . . you know, so you won't be too disappointed or anything."

Dad glanced back at the boys. "Still, there's no harm in trying, Avi. Anything's possible."

Reuven leaned against the door and stared out of his window. He'd never stop being amazed by his little brother. Where did he get the nerve? Thinking he could be picked for All-Stars in his rookie year. Reuven had never even given it a moment's thought last year. Not if you counted thinking and dreaming as two separate things.

This year could be different, though. Reuven had practiced pitching all year against a plastic backstop in their backyard. He'd lifted weights four days a week to develop his upper body, and he'd studied books about pitching. He certainly didn't "expect" to make All-Stars this year. *Expect* was such a very big word. He didn't expect it—but, maybe, just maybe . . .

Reuven was glad when his dad finally pulled into the parking lot of the Silver Spring Yeshiva Junior and Senior High School for Boys. That would stop all the talk about All-Stars, which was making his stomach turn into a tight knot. He and Avi scrambled out of the car.

This was a school for Orthodox Jewish boys, and the students all wore traditional Jewish skullcaps and dressed in white shirts and dark pants. No jeans. No T-shirts. That just wouldn't be considered proper.

"Wait, guys!" Dad called after them. "What time is

practice today?"

"Five, Dad," Avi yelled back. "Can we make it? We don't want to be late on the first day."

"It'll be close, but I'll get you there." Dad waved and started to pull away.

"Can we ask our teachers to let us out early, Dad? Just ten minutes?"

Mr. Silver pulled close to the curb again, took off his glasses, rubbed his eyes, and put them back on. "All right. But just today. And only if you're finished early."

Dad finally drove off, and Reuven and Avi started walking again.

"Mr. Myer is always done early. What about Mr. Graham, Reuven? Do you think he'll finish early?"

"I don't know. I'll ask."

The boys stepped into the school's crowded hallway. There was only one. One wide, gray hallway with doors lined up on both sides. Every room in the school looked the same, except for the one very long room that took up almost half of one side of the building. That was the *bet midrash*—where they gathered to pray twice a day.

"So, can you get out of Mr. Graham's class early, Reuven?"

"I don't know," he finally answered. "Ninth grade is lots harder than eighth. And Mr. Graham talks for the whole period, sometimes."

"Well, try, anyway," Avi called as they turned in opposite directions to find their lockers.

Reuven shoved through a clump of boys and started spinning the dial on his combination lock.

"Hey, Reuven. How did you do on the math problems? Did you get?"

"Hi, Simcha," Reuven answered, without looking up. "I got them, but my mom helped me."

Simcha's locker was ten away from his, but Simcha always appeared at Reuven's side first thing in the morning.

"I can show you at lunch," Reuven offered.

"Hi, Reuven! Hi, Russian!" a voice interrupted.

Reuven gave a backward wave at Peretz without even bothering to look up. He knew it was Peretz. When you had been with the same group of guys since kindergarten, it was easy to recognize voices.

"Hi, Peretz," Simcha called, waving at the crowd of boys moving toward the *bet midrash.*

Simcha hadn't been part of this group very long. In fact, he'd only arrived here two years ago from Russia. Most of the guys still thought of him as a new boy, and many still called him Russian. Simcha never seemed to mind.

"Yes, good. We will work at lunch. I could not get all of the problems."

Reuven nodded because they almost always worked on something together at lunch. He crammed his books and lunch into his locker, took his prayer book off the top shelf, and headed for the bet midrash.

At lunch, Avi's friend, Itzi, tapped Reuven's shoulder.

"Avi says you're pitching this year."

"Avi talks too much." Reuven concentrated on what he was doing.

"How come you don't pitch for us?"

" 'Cause we don't have a team."

"I meant at lunchtime." Itzi persisted. "Are you gonna pitch for us?"

"You wouldn't want him to," Avi called out. "He throws too hard. Nobody here could even hit him." Reuven blushed a little amazed that his kid brother would have said that about him.

"Hey, Reuven," Avi called as he was leaving the lunchroom. "Remember, to talk to Mr. Graham."

Reuven nodded and gave a quick wave to his brother. But by the time the last period of the day had finally arrived and it was time for Mr. Graham's class, Reuven wasn't so sure he'd be able to get the chance to ask about leaving early.

He stepped into the room and saw piles of papers on the desk and three boys lined up waiting to talk to Mr. Graham. Reuven joined the line, watched the clock, and tapped his foot, but the other boys just wouldn't talk any faster. One argued about the last test, and another one gave a wild excuse for having late homework. Reuven never heard what the third one wanted because the bell rang.

"Let me catch you two guys after class. Okay?"

"Sure, Mr. Graham," Reuven mumbled.

"Well, boys."

When Mr. Graham began with "Well, boys," it meant an important announcement was coming.

"You're in ninth grade now. More than halfway through ninth grade, really. And by now, you know it isn't as easy as seventh and eighth grades were. Especially not in my class. Right?"

The class laughed, but it was a nervous laugh.

Mr. Graham leaned back against his desk, propping one foot on the edge of the chair in front of him.

"But the good part about ninth grade is that you're now eligible for Senior Honor Roll. Making Honor Roll is something to be proud of, and I've been asked to recommend ninth graders for it. The rules only require a B average, but I want to look for something extra."

Reuven had made Junior Honor Roll in both seventh and eight grades, and he knew he had better than a B average. Whatever extra Mr. Graham wanted, Reuven felt ready to do it.

"I've decided to assign a research paper," Mr. Graham continued.

"I want you to find an interesting way to approach your subject, and I want the papers typed. You can use the school's computers if you need to."

Mr. Graham let the boys think this over.

"Now everyone listen carefully," he went on. "I want these papers turned in on time. The due date is in the guidelines and . . ." Mr. Graham looked right at the boy who had tried to offer the wild excuse for his late homework. "If the paper is even one day late, I won't give you an A, and I certainly won't recommend you for Honor Roll."

Reuven leaned back in his chair and relaxed. He didn't mind writing papers, and he always did things on time.

Mr. Graham passed out reference materials, then strolled between the rows of desks, peeking over shoulders and giving ideas for topics. Reuven thought this might be a good time to finally ask if he could leave a little early.

"You're certainly one of the boys that I have my eye on for a recommendation," Mr. Graham said before Reuven could speak. "Your work has been excellent this year. I'm looking forward to a great paper from you."

Reuven felt a warm rush flooding his face.

"Oh. Was there something you wanted to ask me?"

"Um. No. It wasn't important."

Reuven glanced at the clock as Mr. Graham moved on to the next person. It wouldn't have mattered, anyway. The bell rang a few minutes later.

Reuven dashed to his locker, then out to the parking lot. Avi was already waiting in the car, leaning out the window, waving for him to hurry.

"Wouldn't Mr. Graham let you out early?" Avi demanded as Reuven tumbled into the backseat.

"I never got a chance to ask."

"Great. So you never even talked to him," Avi folded his arms in front of his chest and stared straight ahead. "First practice of the season and we're going to be late. Thanks a lot."

Mr. Silver knew a shortcut, and he got them to their first Tigers' practice with a minute to spare. Reuven and Avi barreled out of the car, raced down a small hill to the field, and found five other boys sitting on the dugout bench.

Avi plopped down at one end of the bench and Reuven at the other. No one spoke. Except for an occasional twitch or scratch and Reuven's feet pumping up and down like runaway pistons, all was still.

Reuven took in a deep breath. He smelled mowed-down onion grass, the stink of new pear blossoms, and bubble gum. When Reuven leaned forward to see whose jaw was churning, he spotted a tall, blond kid with a giant pink bubble billowing out from his face.

The bubble popped, and Reuven turned toward the field again where a sea of golden sparkles ricocheted off the pebbles of the skin infield. It was pretty to look at, but it sure wasn't going to feel good on elbows and knees if you had to slide. Reuven knew he would slide, anyway. If he got the chance. A few pebbles wouldn't stop him.

A sudden whistle interrupted the silence.

"Shwe-e-e-t-shwu!"

It was a high-pitched, off-key whistle. The kind that you made by pulling your lips in a wide, thin line and pushing the sound out through a tiny slit at the side of your mouth. It was the kind of whistle that sliced through the air and demanded attention.

"Shwe-e-e-t-shwu!"

Seven heads bobbed up, turning this way and that. Avi pointed to a young man hustling in from the parking lot.

"Is that our coach?"

He wasn't much bigger than most of the boys and had straight brown hair spreading out in a million directions from the back of his baseball cap.

"Sorry, guys. Traffic." He took a moment to catch his breath. "Didn't any of you guys bring a ball? When I arrive, I like to see my team busy warming up." He set down a bucket filled with baseballs. "I'm Mark Andrews. Played in college and I've done a few years of coaching, so I think we can have a great season together. Let me take a few minutes to tell everybody how I approach baseball.

"I want us all to have a good time, but I also want you to push yourselves to do your very best. It's important to do your absolute best at everything you do. That's how I am in life. I don't just want to emphasize competition, but there's lots of competition in life, and baseball is no different. Does everybody know about All-Stars?"

Avi nodded. Reuven stared down at his feet.

"Being an All-Star is a great honor. Not just for yourself but for the team you represent. I watch my boys right from the first day. I'm going to judge you on your work ethic during practices, your sportsmanship, and your team spirit as much as I judge you on your skills. Okay. Let's pair off and get those arms warmed up."

Avi leaped up and was the first to reach into the bucket and scoop out a ball. He turned to the boy next to him, and the two of them moved out onto the field. Reuven stared after them. By the time he looked back toward the bench, the other four boys had already paired off.

Reuven grabbed a ball, then wondered what to do with it. He tossed it up and caught it. The coach was the only other person left who wasn't on the field, and he was busy dumping helmets and catcher's gear out of a large canvas bag. Reuven tossed the ball up and caught it again.

"Just call me Mark," the coach said, turning toward Reuven. "Come on. Let's you and me warm up."

Mark headed out onto the field with Reuven following. They took up position, and Mark sailed the ball toward Reuven, slow and easy. No challenge at all. Reuven stretched his glove out with all the confidence of someone who had spent endless hours practicing fielding—and missed. The ball sailed past him, rolling solemnly out toward the fence. Reuven gave chase, then hustled back.

"We can stand a little closer," Mark said, smiling.

"Nah. It's all right. I just—uh—it was the sun."

That didn't explain why everybody else was catching without any trouble. But Reuven didn't want to admit that he was so busy being annoyed at Avi for pairing off with someone else and leaving him the only one without a partner that he couldn't concentrate. It was just easier to blame the sun.

"What's your name?"

"Reuven Silver."

"Which brother are you?"

"Older."

"Mmm . . . and you like third base and pitching. See? I read the sheets." Mark laughed.

While they worked, Mark talked about playing in leagues when he was a kid and how he used to enjoy practices a lot more than he ever enjoyed the games. Every six or seven throws, he backed up and motioned for Reuven to back up, too.

"You have a good arm. Can you make the throw to first?"

"You mean from third? Well, yeah, I guess."

"Good. We'll give it a try later."

"Shwe-e-e-t-shwu!" Mark's whistle got the attention of the pair of boys next to them. He took one boy's place and that boy moved over to throw with Reuven.

For the next half hour, Mark moved around until he'd had a chance to throw with every boy. Four more boys joined the field as they practiced, making a total of eleven on the team. At last, Mark whistled one more time and motioned for the team to join him at the bench.

"Hey, you guys are looking great. We've got lots of strong arms here. Now, I want everybody to take your favorite infield position. No more than two or three of you at each position, and we'll try some fielding practice. Do you all know one another's names?"

The boys looked at one another, shrugged their shoulders, and shook their heads. So, Mark went down the list. He remembered everybody. Reuven was amazed. By the time Mark had finished telling a little about one boy and was introducing the next, Reuven could hardly remember the name of the one he'd just introduced.

One boy, Henry Fuller, had been on Reuven's team last year. He'd gotten a lot taller, and Reuven didn't recognize him until Mark said his name. Bubblegum Boy's name was really Steve, and he liked third or left. Avi had paired off with Dan, who was the shortest on the team. By the time they took the field, those were the only names that Reuven could remember. He'd have to check with Avi.

Reuven chose third base. Avi and Dan chose shortstop. Steve also took third base and placed himself in front of Reuven, even though Reuven had gotten there first.

Pop! A pink bubble flashed and disappeared. Up close, Reuven could see tiny pink specks all around Steve's face.

"I'm Steve and you're . . ."

"Reuven."

"Yeah. Funny name. So, what's your batting average?

Mine's about .300."

"I don't think mine's that good," Reuven mumbled.

"Yeah, but I stink in the field. What about you? You any good in the field?"

"Well. Yeah. Nah. I don't stink." Then Reuven laughed. "I mean not usually or anything. I have my days. You know . . . when I stink."

Steve laughed, too.

"Hey, Reuven!" Avi yelled. "Dan says he was an All-Star last year. Do you remember him?"

"Heads up, guys!" Mark called, letting the boys know that he was ready to start.

So, Dan was an All-Star last year. Reuven focused on Mark. Well, this was a new year. A fresh chance. And Reuven intended to make the most of it.

Mark had a bucket of balls and a bat. He began with third base, hitting a quick grounder out that way. Steve was supposed to snare the ball and fire it to first. He didn't. His glove was a foot away from the ground as the ball shot by him, rolling out to right field.

Reuven watched it scoot by. Steve was right. His fielding did stink. Maybe he could hit, but he sure wasn't going to be much competition for third base.

"Yo, Reuven!" Mark called. "You're supposed to back him up. Let's try another one, Steve. Everyone get in the game now. I don't want anybody standing around watching balls roll by, even if it's not your turn."

Great, Reuven thought. Steve misses and I get yelled at.

Steve missed the next two balls, but Reuven made sure he was ready to field them. He moved up a little closer to Steve after fielding the second one and whispered, "Try to bend your knees on grounders. You can't get your glove down if you don't bend your knees."

Steve nodded and did bend his knees a little more on the next one. He made the pickup just fine that time, but bounced his throw to first.

"Oh, well," Steve said, as he backed away to let Reuven move into position. "At least, I got it."

Reuven took a moment to slap hands with him. "Don't worry about it. That's a long throw. It just takes practice."

"Nice backup," Mark called to Reuven before moving on to the shortstop position. "I hope everyone else was paying attention. Practice like you're playing a game, boys. Practice like you're playing a game."

Reuven looked down and kicked at the grass. This was how Dad had taught Avi and him to practice. He was just doing what came naturally. Still, it was nice to have the coach notice.

Mark sent the next ball to Avi who fielded it cleanly, as did the second baseman. Reuven's turn.

Mark hit him a shot. It skittered across the dirt infield and took a sharp hop toward second base. Reuven made a short, quick jump to his left, placing his glove on the ground just as Dad had taught him. He scooped the ball into his glove, set his feet, and fired to first. Straight, quick, and right into the first baseman's glove.

"Yow!" The boy on first had it for a split second before the ball skipped over the top of his glove to shoot off into foul territory.

"Hey, nice throw!" Mark called. "You gotta do it just a little softer, but I AM impressed."

Reuven took in a great gulp of spring air and relaxed. He loved fielding. Really loved it. Loved the suspense of not knowing where the ball would be coming from. Loved turning the work entirely over to his body, trusting his instincts to pull him to the ball. He loved making the throws and watching the ball sail to its intended target.

Dan shifted over to first base after a while and never once dropped a ball that Reuven directed to his glove. No matter how hard Reuven threw it.

Avi did well, too. Avi was a natural shortstop. He was lean, angular, and could spring in any direction.

After Mark had seen everybody's fielding, they moved on to batting practice. Mark pitched almost a full bucket of balls to each boy. Reuven hit well enough. Avi hit a little better than Reuven, and Henry was pretty good. Dan didn't show much for a former All-Star.

It was Steve who really stood out. Steve sure had told the truth about his hitting. He could hit a ton. He must have sent four or five balls almost to the back fence. Reuven was going to have to ask Dad about spending more time at the batting cage.

Practice officially ended, but Mark wanted a chance to look over the pitchers. Reuven and Avi stayed. Henry stayed. Mike and Pete stayed. Mark wanted each boy to pitch until he had put out three batters.

Mike and Pete struggled. In fact, Pete never even got his three outs.

Avi was next. Avi struck out the first batter on three pitches. Of course, he was pitching to Pete who was one of their worst hitters.

"OK! Now we're seeing some pitching," Mark called.

Reuven couldn't believe it. Mark had to be smarter than that. He could remember all those names and facts, but he couldn't figure out that Avi had just lucked out and gotten the worst hitter on the team for his first try?

Henry batted next, and he put Avi's very first pitch downtown. To the fence. Thank-you, Henry.

"Too bad, Avi," Reuven thought. But then, not many people even tried out for pitcher in their first year, so Avi really couldn't complain.

"Man, that thing musta had wings." Mark laughed. "It was a good strike, anyway, Avi. Don't let it bother you. Throwing strikes is the important thing. You're not going to have too many hitters like Henry in this league."

Reuven hit next. He piddled a grounder on Avi's second pitch. It wasn't a great hit, but he sure was glad that his kid brother hadn't struck him out.

Mike hit one right back to Avi, and Pete flailed away at obvious balls for another easy out. Reuven was up next.

Reuven's first pitch was fast and wild. Mark didn't say a word. Henry, at the plate, shifted in a little closer.

Reuven focused on Mark's glove. He dug his heel into the hole in the mound that was serving as their rubber. He reared back and released.

That one felt right. It felt the way a good pitch was supposed to feel, like the ball was an extension of his own arm, reaching distances he couldn't reach.

Thwack. Reuven's snapped into Mark's glove.

"Hey! Was that a hundred miles an hour or what?" Henry said, shaking his head.

"YES, Reuven," Mark called out. "Great speed. Excellent placement. Do it again."

Reuven did do it again, and two pitches later, it was Avi's turn at bat. Avi always swung at low balls, and Reuven knew he could get him out on three low pitches. But he needed to show Mark strikes. The two brothers had hit off each other enough times that it was always dangerous to serve Avi strikes. He could get lucky and take Reuven downtown, just like Henry had done to Avi.

Reuven had no choice. He had to show Mark that he could throw consistent strikes.

Avi popped the first pitch foul. The second one, he swung on too late. He caught the third pitch perfectly and made a big show of running the bases. He waved his fists in the air and danced from base to base. Reuven heard some laughter from out in the field, but he didn't see what was so funny. Not at all. Pete and Mike were easy outs to end Reuven's tryout.

"Yo, Reuven. Do you happen to have a curveball?"

Reuven turned to face Mark. "Uh—no. Not yet. I mean my dad says I'm too young. But I've been reading up on it."

"That's okay. Forget it. I agree with your dad. I've seen kids get injured that way. You've got plenty enough speed to get your share of outs. But some boys do throw it. I just thought I'd ask."

Henry pitched next. Reuven remembered that Henry had pitched last year, too. He seemed to have lost some speed, but his accuracy was still good. Reuven hung behind the backstop studying Henry's form. His last two pitches did something very strange.

"Hey, were those curveballs I just saw?" Mark wanted to know.

Henry nodded.

"Okay, guys. Thanks for giving me all this extra time. This has been a great practice. Reuven and Henry are going to be my starting pitchers. Mike and Avi will be relievers. Pete, let's you and I do some work together before we call you a pitcher."

Pete shrugged.

"Reuven, you've got a powerhouse of an arm. I AM impressed."

Reuven was careful not to smile. He didn't want to show off.

Avi got to the parking lot first where Dad and Mom were waiting. Avi launched in telling them how well he had fielded and that his hitting had been okay, too.

"There's one guy on the team that really hits good. You were talking to him, Reuven."

"Steve. His name is Steve. He seems pretty nice."

"But he really can hit, can't he?"

"Yeah. Can we go to the batting cage, Dad?"

"What's the story on pitching?" Dad asked. "Any decisions yet?"

"I got picked," Reuven answered with a wide grin. "I'm a starter. And Avi's a reliever. Not bad for a rookie."

"Wow," Mom chimed in. "A starter and a reliever. You both must have done really great."

Just then, Coach Andrews pulled up next to their car. He nodded to Mr. and Mrs. Silver and smiled at Reuven and Avi who were standing between the two cars. "Should be a great season, boys. I'm looking forward to it."

Reuven was looking forward to it, too, but before he could say another word, Henry strolled by.

"Henry!" Coach Andrews called. "Work on that curve. I'll probably start you in the first game."

Reuven froze with his hand on the car door. He didn't even wave as Mark drove off.

Suddenly, it felt like his heart had just dropped out of his body and crashed to the ground. Why did the coach say that stuff about his powerhouse arm? Curveballs seemed to be the only thing that mattered in this league. Curveballs. And Reuven didn't have one.

4

"Want me to show you how this works?"

Simcha peered over Reuven's shoulder.

"Okay. So you click on this, and then type in 'Civil War,' and then"—Reuven pointed at the computer screen in front of him—"it shows you where to find your books." He flipped the switch on the printer and waited for the paper to slowly roll out.

"I never see this before." Simcha leaned in closer, but carefully avoided touching anything.

"You had libraries in Russia, didn't you?"

"No computers. I never see computer in a library before."

Reuven shrugged, then led Simcha into the book stacks to show him how to find what he wanted. They were here on a field trip. Mr. Graham had led the class on the two-block walk from the yeshiva to this public library so the boys could gather materials for their term papers.

Yeshiva boys were crowded into every aisle with history books. They gathered in clumps of two or three, opened books, studied tables of contents, whispered, and poked one another in the ribs. There was some giggling.

"Here." Reuven handed Simcha his list of books. "I need something from over there. I'll be back in a minute."

Reuven slipped away. He knew exactly what he wanted and where to get it. He grabbed his book, then scooted into the line waiting for checkout.

It was an awfully long line for the middle of the day. Two women with small children clinging to their legs waited ahead of Reuven, each holding mile high stacks of picture books.

Reuven glanced around the room. His classmates were wandering in the tall book stacks. He should be able to check this out and hustle back without any questions.

One woman stepped up to the desk, and Reuven inched forward. Then he saw Simcha waving, grinning, and heading his way.

Reuven shifted the book he was holding to his other side, the side that Simcha couldn't see. He tried to look thoroughly bored.

"You have your books already?"

"Mmm, not exactly. Just one so far. I'm getting this one, then I'll look for more."

"But why do that?" Simcha asked. "Then you have to stand on line twice. In Russia, we always stand on lines. I don't like to stand on lines, now."

Simcha moved to Reuven's left, so Reuven switched the book to his right side. Simcha circled to Reuven's right, just as he slipped the book back to his left.

"Why you don't want me to see that? What is it?"

Simcha reached for the book, and Reuven spun to avoid him, bumping into one of the little kids clinging to the woman in front of him. The mother gave him a squinched-up-eyebrows, tight-pressed-lips sort of look. Reuven mumbled an apology just as Simcha grabbed the book from his hand.

"Guide to Pitching Techniques," Simcha read out loud. "Why are you getting this? What is your paper?"

"Baseball during the Civil War."

"Wow! That's good." Simcha flipped a few pages. "I don't see 'Civil War' in here."

"I'm kidding," Reuven said with a sigh. "I'm really doing the Battle of Gettysburg. This is for something else."

Finally, Reuven checked out his book, stowed it in his bag, then pointed Simcha back toward the history section. Once they had collected the books they needed, the boys settled at a table to start making notes.

"Did you make home runs?" Simcha whispered as he worked.

"Huh?"

"Avi told me about your baseball practice. Did you make home runs?"

"You don't make home runs in practices." Reuven stopped writing and looked up. "It doesn't count, anyway.

You're supposed to be working on technique. Doesn't matter about making home runs."

"He said he made home runs."

Reuven snorted. "Avi's a hot dog."

Simcha stared at Reuven for a few minutes, then hunched over his paper and continued scratching out notes. Finally, he put down his pen to stare at Reuven.

"But I thought hot dog was thing to eat. In bread."

Reuven exploded in a loud laugh. Simcha's face turned the color of beet soup, and Reuven felt bad about that. He usually tried not to make fun of Simcha's struggles with English. This time he couldn't help himself.

"It also means someone who acts like a hot dog."

Simcha still had his eyebrows drawn close in a tight squiggle of confusion, but Reuven was too busy laughing to explain more. Before Simcha could probe any deeper into the mysteries of English slang, a bustling crowd of kids noisily entered the library.

Reuven looked up; then, suddenly, his face went white. He spun around in his chair to avoid being seen and sent a pile of books clattering to the floor.

"Hey! I know you," one of the boys in the crowd called out. "Reuben. Right? Good arm. Right?"

It was Steve, from the Tigers. Reuven smiled and nodded.

"You go to school around here, too? That private school?"

By then, a group of Steve's friends had crowded in around him.

"Hey, this is a guy from my team," Steve announced. "Name's Reuben. He's a good third baseman. Right, Reuben?"

Simcha nudged him. Reuven had no choice.

"It's Reuven." He pronounced it carefully, emphasizing the second syllable and the *v*.

"Sorry. Roo-Vane."

Steve said it in a way that made Reuven's name sound really funny. Then he said it again making the "Roo" part sound like a mooing cow. His friends laughed. A few imitated the way Steve had said Reuven's name. Then they wandered off to different corners of the library. Reuven could hear a few "Roo-Vanes" drifting around the library, followed by laughter and shushing from the librarians. Steve still stood by their table.

"That's a Jewish cap, right?" Steve pointed to the small black cap on Reuven's head. "I didn't know you were Jewish."

"It's called a *kippah*. Some people say *yarmulke.*"

Reuven reached up and adjusted his kippah a little. That was an automatic reflex with him. Reuven had been taught to wear his kippah at all times to remind himself that God was always with him. Even when he played baseball. But then he made sure that it was covered by his baseball cap. Now that Steve had seen it, he would probably ask a million embarrassing questions.

"So what are you guys doing here?"

"We have to do a term paper," Reuven answered,

relieved to be talking about something ordinary. "Our teacher brought us here to get books."

"Man, this must be term-paper season. That's why we're here, too. I think all the teachers find this stuff in some teachers' magazine. The weather gets good, and they all start assigning term papers. Anyway, I gotta go before I get into any trouble. See you at practice."

Steve waved and went off to find his friends. Reuven turned back to his own work, hoping Simcha would just let it drop. He didn't.

"Your baseball is not Jewish baseball?"

"No such thing as Jewish baseball," Reuven mumbled.

"I meant your team is not Jewish people. Right?"

"Right. It's just anybody. I don't know who's Jewish or who isn't."

"That isn't problem here?"

Reuven shrugged and continued taking notes.

"In Russia, would be problem. We never tell people we are Jewish, but everybody seem to know, anyway. Maybe was my curly hair."

Simcha twiddled his curly hair. He wrapped one dark curl at a time around his finger, then pulled his hand away, letting the hair spring back to its rightful place. "Other kids didn't like me. They don't like that I'm Jewish. They did mean things."

Reuven couldn't think of any answer for that, so he went on working. Simcha hunched down over his work, too, but popped up every time Steve's booming voice sounded from some corner of the library.

"Hey, it's okay," Reuven finally said, putting his hand on Simcha's shoulder. "People ask embarrassing questions sometimes, but nobody bothers anybody. It's okay to be just about anything here. Don't worry about it."

Simcha didn't look entirely reassured, but at least, he stopped jumping every time Steve or his friends made noise. On the way back, Reuven strolled as slowly as he thought Mr. Graham would allow. He loved days like this with just enough breeze to feel clean against his face.

There was another reason why Reuven didn't want to hurry. A group of girls from the other yeshiva campus was walking toward them on the opposite side of the street. The two campuses were far enough apart so that the boys and girls rarely ran into one another. But it looked like they were heading for the library, too.

Steve was right. This did seem to be term-paper season, and the teachers at the boys' school must have forgotten to coordinate library day with the teachers from the girls' school. Reuven wondered why they couldn't have gone about a half hour earlier.

Not that he would have talked to any of the girls. His rabbis wouldn't like that. But maybe some really pretty girl would have just happened to have a question, and he might have just happened to be standing right by the book that the pretty girl needed. Then that would be okay—sort of.

Especially if it had been the one with the black curly

hair.

Reuven shook his head because he knew he shouldn't be daydreaming about girls. Just toss those thoughts right out of your head, he thought. Baseball. Now there was something you could daydream about.

And this day—this day with the cool breeze and the sweet-smelling air—was just about perfect for thinking about baseball. He imagined the wind whooshing past him as he ran the bases. He thought about the crowd cheering and his name ringing out. He thought he could almost hear it. And then, just as he and Simcha turned to walk up the path to the school's front door, Reuven did hear his name ring out. Loud and clear.

"Roo-Vane! Roo-Vane!"

A car sped past, and Reuven spun around just in time to spot a hand waving out the window. He froze in place wondering who else might have heard that. His friends in school? The girls who were coming closer on the sidewalk?

"Hey, wasn't that Steve?" Avi called from the front door of the yeshiva where he was waiting for his next class.

Well, Avi heard it. That was for sure.

"How come you didn't wave?"

"Didn't have time," Reuven grumbled. "And I saw him already. At the library."

"Still could have waved. Where does he go to school?"

"I don't know. I didn't ask."

"What grade's he in?"

"Didn't ask that either."

"Boy, you are the friendly one, aren't you?"

Reuven hurried past Avi into the school's crowded hallway with Simcha just a step behind. He hadn't taken more than a few steps inside the building before it started.

"Roo-Vane."

It seemed that everyone else had heard it, too.

"Roo-Vane."

His name echoed from every corner of the long hallway, from behind locker doors, from classrooms. When Steve had screamed his name out that car window, he had stretched out the "Roo" part into a long, undulating sound like the moo of a cow. Now that same mooing-rooing was bouncing all around the yeshiva, intermixed with laughter.

Reuven expected that sort of thing from THEM, but not from these kids. Not from kids whose names were just as strange to other people's ears as Reuven's. He didn't expect Moshe or Yuri or Peretz to make fun of his name.

"What's the noise, gentlemen?" One of the rabbis appeared in a doorway, and the hall quickly settled into quiet. Everyone stopped what they were doing and stood politely. "Let's get to class now. The bell will ring any minute."

That ended the mooing-rooing. All the boys finished gathering books from their lockers and hurried off to their classrooms.

"Hey, Simcha," Avi called from one end of the hallway as the crowd began to thin out. "Why don't you come to our game this Sunday? Time you learned a little about American baseball."

"Well, sure. I guess. I'll ask my parents."

Simcha went off to his class, but Reuven stayed, glowering at his brother.

"Why did you do that?"

"Why not? He's your friend, isn't he? I thought you'd want to show off a little for a friend."

"I could ask him if I wanted. I don't need your help."

"Sure you do. You're too shy to ask. I did you a favor."

Avi started to walk off.

"Wait a minute," Reuven demanded, angry more that his little brother had called him shy than anything else. "What do you mean about showing off? What am I supposed to be showing off?"

"Your pitching, of course. You're the best pitcher on our team. Don't you know that?"

"I'm not the best. I'm not even going to start because I can't throw a curve."

"You don't need a curve. You have that eight-million-mile-an-hour fastball. I wish I had one." Avi paused at the door to his classroom. "And I bet you will start," he called over his shoulder.

Reuven stood motionless, staring down the now empty hallway. How could the most annoying kid brother ever invented say something so nice? While he pondered that thought, the bell rang, and Reuven realized he was going to be tardy for the first time this year.

5

Reuven finished buttoning his shirt, then turned to face the tower of books blocking the path to his bedroom door. He thought he'd gathered them all up last night but noticed now that there were a few runaways scattered about the floor and one hiding under the bed. Only its frayed spine poked through the crumpled pile of bedspread and blanket.

Stepping carefully around it all, Reuven headed downstairs for breakfast. He paused just long enough to bang on Avi's closed door—in case he was still asleep.

It was Saturday. The Jewish Sabbath. Today, Reuven and his family would walk the three miles to their small synagogue.

The family ate quickly and headed out with the night's chill clinging to the morning air, tweaking Reuven's nose and sparking a little twitching and sniffling. Still, the sun was trying hard, so Reuven let his jacket flop open to welcome the first warmth of the day. He settled into a comfortable pace and was ready to talk baseball.

"Dad," Reuven began. "How do you think the Orioles'—"

"I think I'm going to be catching," Avi interrupted.

"—pitching is going to be this year? I read—"

"Or shortstop. But no one else wants to catch."

"Guys! Just a minute." Dad clapped his hands over his ears. "I can't hear you both at the same time. Okay. Avi, first. Something about catching?"

"But why should Avi . . ." Reuven started to protest.

"I said . . ." Avi paused, waiting for quiet. "I said . . . no one wants to catch Reuven. They're all afraid of him."

"Who said that?" Reuven asked genuinely surprised.

"Everyone. Cause you throw too hard. I'm the only one that can catch you. And I'm going to pick someone off second."

"I never heard anyone . . ."

"You think you can make that throw?" Dad asked with a smile.

"I've been practicing it. Mark said I could try if I got the chance."

"Now, what did you want to say?" Dad turned to Reuven.

"Hmmm?" Reuven was still thinking about what Avi had said. "Oh, yes. About Orioles' pitching this year. I read they picked up this really great pitcher from the minors."

"I don't know, Reuven. I hadn't read that. But what about your pitching? So you think you'll be pitching tomorrow?"

"Yep," Avi chimed in. "The coach told me so. Reuven's pitching and I'm catching."

"That'll be fun to watch," Dad said. "What's wrong, Reuven? Aren't you excited about it?"

"I'm excited about pitching. It's just that I thought I had a chance to be the starter."

"You're not starting?" Dad asked.

"Nope." Reuven shook his head. "Haven't got a curve."

"You're going to do great, anyway, son," Dad reassured him. "You have nothing to worry about."

Reuven trudged on in silence, staring down at his feet.

"Hey, Reuven," Avi called out. "Isn't that Henry?"

Reuven was deep in thought. He was thinking about throwing harder than most other boys his age. And he hadn't even realized that the other boys didn't want to catch him. That sounded kind of bad, but really it was a good thing. Throwing hard was good.

"Over there, Reuven. That's Henry and Steve. Come on, let's catch up to them."

Reuven finally looked up. It WAS Henry and Steve heading in the direction of a local school ground, and Avi had already taken off jogging toward them. The three were chatting at the corner when Reuven finally caught up. The very first word he heard was "curveball."

"Henry's going to practice his curveball," Avi announced. "I told him you didn't have one."

"And I'm going to practice hitting it," Steve said, grinning.

"I heard it wasn't such a good idea at our age to be throwing curves." Reuven said, knowing how dumb that sounded. "You should be careful."

"Yeah. That's what my dad says. It's okay. I've been throwing it for a while."

"So. You want to come along?" Steve asked. "How come you're all dressed up?"

"Uh. We have somewhere to go," Reuven stammered.

"We're going to synagogue," Avi answered at the same time, shooting Reuven a puzzled look.

"Oh. Well, see you tomorrow then."

Mr. and Mrs. Silver arrived at the corner just as Steve and Henry waved and went on their way.

"The one on the left is Henry, Dad." Reuven pointed at their disappearing backs. "He's our starter."

"Ahh. He must be awfully good, then, if the coach thinks he's better than you."

"I don't know about that, exactly. But he throws a curve."

Reuven hoped that Dad would get the point and, finally, offer to teach him how to throw one. But Dad just ignored him and went on talking to Mom about unimportant things. Baseball wasn't even mentioned.

When they got to synagogue, Dad took his usual seat

on the men's side and Mom sat with the women. Reuven started to follow his father when he noticed that Avi was lingering next to the curtain that separated the two sections of seats. He had pulled back one section of the curtain so that he could look through into the women's side.

"What are you doing?"

"Shhh. Come here." Avi crooked his finger beckoning Reuven to join him.

"What?" Reuven peeked around his brother.

"Isn't that Rachel Cohen?"

"Where?"

"Second row."

"Yeah. So?"

"So, she's cute, don't you think."

Reuven took a step back, then moved forward and looked again into the women's section. "You're not supposed to be doing this. Go sit down."

"Yeah. Yeah." Avi pushed past Reuven and went to take his seat.

Reuven shook his head. That Avi. What was he thinking? But before Reuven headed for his own seat, he reached up to push the curtain back the way it was supposed to be. He glanced around, and no one seemed to be paying attention to him. So, he took one more quick look and couldn't help noticing how Rachel's hair—a mass of black curls—seemed to dance as she turned a little from side to side.

Reuven took his seat and hurried to catch up with the opening prayers. When they were finished, it was time to read the Torah. The rabbi scanned the congregation to pick out someone who would have the job of calling out the Hebrew names of other men to take part in the reading.

Reuven knew it was a great honor to be selected for this job. He also knew how much he hated speaking in front of the congregation. He had known most of these people all of his life, and he knew very well the prayers and the rituals. He could say it all in his head, perfectly. But as soon as he was called upon to do it in front of the congregation, he would stammer and stutter and forget everything.

Reuven stared down at his book, as if he had not quite finished saying some of the opening prayers.

"Reuven?" the rabbi asked softly.

Reuven kept his eyes on his book. There was a pause, a long silent pause, until, finally, he heard his father's voice.

"Maybe Avi. Avi will do it."

Reuven sighed quietly, to himself. He could breathe again. Even if it was embarrassing having his little brother do something that he couldn't.

Avi took his place in front of the congregation and called out the names loud and clear. Every once in a while, he said a name wrong. The rabbi corrected him, and Avi repeated it. He never even blushed. Like it didn't even matter when he made mistakes.

When the reading of the Torah was complete, the rabbi picked Reuven for the job of lifting the Torah. This time, Reuven didn't look down or pretend not to hear. This was a job that Reuven enjoyed doing.

The Torah is much heavier then most people realize. Just lifting it at all requires a strong person, and at this point in the service, the Torah has to be held up high enough so that everyone can see the writing. That means the person lifting it has to hold the two heavy wooden handles wide apart, while lifting the Torah high in the air.

That was not an easy job. Many men just weren't strong enough to do this. The rabbi knew who could and couldn't lift the Torah and was careful not to embarrass anyone. Mr. Silver could do it, and everyone knew that Reuven could do it, too.

He opened the scroll the right amount, set his feet, and pretended for a moment that he was lifting weights at home. The Torah rose as he stretched his arms straight, and everyone in the congregation rose, too, because anytime the Torah was lifted, people stood to show respect.

Reuven turned to let everyone see the writing. From the front, he could see into both sides of the room. As he spun toward the women's section, he couldn't help noticing Rachel Cohen. For a moment, she seemed to be smiling right at him. But then she turned to say something to her friend sitting next to her, and Reuven wasn't sure if that smile had been meant for him at all.

When the service ended, Dad clapped Reuven on the back and shook his hand.

"Good job, kid. That weight lifting is useful for more than just throwing a baseball, isn't it?"

Other men congratulated him. The women congratulated him. Even Avi congratulated him. Simcha, who also came to their synagogue, joined Reuven and Avi next to a table of snacks.

"How's your history paper coming, Simcha?" Reuven asked.

"Good. It comes good. I write about serfs in Russia same time as American Civil War. Comparing to American slaves."

"Yeah, really? That sounds good. How did you ever think of that?"

"Um, I just think of it. Mr. Graham thinks is good idea, too. Good approach. Mr. Graham say I could win Honor Roll. I hope to win and tell my cousins in Moscow. How is your paper?"

"It's gonna be long. You should see the pile of books I'm using."

"He's not kidding," Avi chimed in. "If he brings any more books up to his room, the floor's gonna cave in."

"Ahh, but you need to have good approach. Not just facts for Honor Roll paper. Mr. Graham tell me that. You have an interesting approach?"

"Not yet, I guess. I haven't exactly thought of one yet. But I will."

Mr. and Mrs. Silver were ready to leave. Avi joined them, and the three waited for Reuven to finish talking to Simcha.

"Like what kind of approach does he want? What would be good for the Battle of Gettysburg?"

"Well, let me think," Simcha started to answer, but Avi stepped between them, tugging at Reuven's arm.

"We've been invited for lunch at the rabbi's. We gotta go."

"Okay. Okay. Just a minute." But Simcha had already walked off to join his own parents. "Hey, Simcha. Maybe I'll call you tomorrow."

"You won't have to. I come to your baseball. Remember?"

"Oh, right." Reuven frowned.

"But I have to ask you favor, anyway," Simcha said as he backed toward his parents. "Paper has to be typed, and we don't have typewriter."

"Sure, sure. You can use my computer."

"Come on, Reuven," Avi nagged.

Reuven let Avi pull him toward the door, then shuffled down the sidewalk a few steps behind his family. His head was buzzing with things he just couldn't stop thinking about. Reuven knew the Sabbath was not supposed to be this way. It wasn't a day to think about work or school or even baseball.

But Reuven couldn't stop thinking about his history paper. He'd felt so sure that he could write a good paper and make Honor Roll. Until he heard Simcha's idea. It really was a good idea. Where was Reuven going to find such a good idea for his paper?

And baseball. Avi was right. The coach had told him over and over how good his pitching was. And how strong his arm was. So how come Henry was going to get to be the starter in their first game of the season? That didn't seem right. Just because Henry could throw a curveball?

Lunch at the rabbi's house was always fun. They had six little kids and usually, while they waited for the meal to be served, Reuven liked watching them tumble around on the floor. Sometimes, they thought it was funny to climb on top of him. He'd always protest, but really he kind of liked it. Today, he didn't feel like playing, so he chose a spot on the sofa right next to Mom. He couldn't help watching them, though, as they grabbed and tickled one another. If you ignored all their giggling, you could almost imagine that they were on a battlefield—fighting one another—face-to-face. Was that how it was at the Battle of Gettysburg?

After lunch, the rabbi led a small discussion. The holiday to celebrate the time when the Jews first heard the Ten Commandments was coming up in a few more weeks. Today, the rabbi spoke about one of the Ten Commandments.

Reuven tried to listen. He tried not to think about Honor Roll or curveballs. The rabbi said it was wrong to covet what other people had, and Reuven wondered how

Simcha had come up with such a good idea for his paper. The rabbi said that we each had what God wanted us to have, and we should take joy in that. Reuven thought about how natural Avi always looked on the pitcher's mound and wondered what it felt like to throw a curve.

"The worst part," the rabbi said, "about coveting, is what it does to you. It makes you feel angry and dissatisfied. People who spend their time wishing for something they don't have forget to enjoy what they do have."

The Silvers got up to leave soon after the rabbi finished his talk. Reuven waited for everyone else to step outside before announcing that he had forgotten his jacket.

"Rabbi," Reuven said as he eased into one sleeve of his jacket. "You know what you were saying? About wanting other people's things? But sometimes, it isn't exactly things people want. Sometimes, people want to be the way somebody else is. More like them. And not like themselves. Is that coveting, do you think?"

"Yes. That's very good, Reuven. That is a type of coveting, too." The rabbi reached over to straighten Reuven's collar. "We always want to be better, don't we? And we can learn from other people. But we don't need to try to be somebody else, right?"

Reuven stood in the rabbi's doorway now and saw his family waiting for him on the sidewalk.

"It's just hard sometimes," he said, looking up at the baby blue sky. "It's hard not to feel jealous."

"Lots of things are hard, Reuven." The rabbi reached

out to shake his hand. "But keep trying. That's all you have to do."

It was almost four o'clock when the Silvers finally set foot in their house again. The long walk and big lunch left everyone tired. Dad slumped into his favorite chair to read the paper, and Avi plopped on the sofa flipping through a magazine. Reuven shut himself in his room and stared out the window. He did not look at the books piled everywhere. It was the Sabbath. No time to think about schoolwork.

Reuven decided it would be all right to just organize things a little. He straightened one already straight pile of books, fished the one book out from under the bed, and gathered up the few that had scattered themselves across the floor.

Guide to Pitching Techniques.

How did that get in with the Civil War books? He could look at that one on the Sabbath. After all, it had nothing to do with schoolwork.

Reuven turned the pages, studying the diagrams as he went. He laid the book open at one page that illustrated a proper windup and stride. After carefully looking over the picture, he practiced a few times moving in slow motion . . . bringing his arms to the center of his chest . . . trying to keep his motion smooth . . . concentrating on where his step landed. Then he tried it once at normal speed, stepped a little too far forward and bumped into the pile of books that he had carefully straightened a few minutes earlier. The whole pile spilled across the floor with a thundering clatter.

"Reuven! What happened? Are you hurt?"

"Nothing, Mom. Something fell over."

Avi poked his head around the door.

"What fell over? The house?"

"You didn't knock."

Avi ignored that and settled himself comfortably on Reuven's bed, fingering the book on pitching techniques.

"Why are you reading this? You already know how to pitch."

"That's a silly thing to say. There's always something to learn. Goes for school, too, you know."

Avi flipped through a few pages, then paused at one with a folded-down corner. He studied that page for a moment. It explained how to throw a curveball.

"Did you do this?" Avi tried to straighten the folded-over corner. "You know Dad doesn't want you trying to throw curves."

"It was already like that. But, anyway, it doesn't look so hard to me. It's mostly just how you grip the ball. I don't know why it's so bad to do it. Lots of guys do. Not just Henry."

"Yeah, but anyway, you don't need to. You've got that fastball that nobody else has. I bet you'll get a ton of strikeouts."

Reuven just stared down at the diagram showing the proper grip for a perfect curve. It didn't look all that hard.

6

The Tigers' first game was Sunday afternoon at two o'clock. Reuven nagged Avi to pass on their usual Sunday morning television programs and get his homework done early. Avi, in turn, nagged Mom and Dad to leave early. When the Silvers pulled up in the parking lot, they were only the third car there.

While Avi squatted down in the almost empty parking lot to tie his cleats, Reuven headed on over to the field. He liked having a few minutes alone before a game. It helped him forget his nervousness and he could imagine . . .

"Shw-e-e-t-shwu"

Reuven jerked right, then left, like a confused compass, until he finally centered himself in the direction of the whistle. The sun glared in his eyes. He squinted hard and was just able to make out a hunched-down shadow by second base. The shadow motioned for him to come over.

Mark was down on his knees pounding the base pad into place. "I want you to start," he said, without even looking up.

"Start? But I thought Henry . . ."

Now, Mark stopped pounding and did look up. He grinned.

"You don't mind starting, do you?"

"No. Sure. I mean that's fine."

"You're the guy with the shotgun arm. I spoke to Henry, already. He understands that you're the stronger pitcher." Mark stretched to his feet, reaching just a little taller than Reuven. "Henry will get plenty of work, too. But I want you to pitch the first four innings. That should get us off to a good start. Warm up with Avi."

By then, Avi had come down from the parking lot. Reuven hustled over to him, gave him the news, then grabbed a ball, and found a good spot to warm up.

Simcha arrived just as Reuven and Avi were starting their warm-up near the spectators' stand. He settled himself on the top row.

Reuven concentrated on their warm-up, but Avi took the time to turn and wave just as Reuven stepped up the speed on his fastball. He was already halfway through his pitching motion when he realized that Avi had looked away. It was too late to stop himself.

"Heads up!" Reuven screamed.

Mark's head jerked up from the bench where he'd been talking to Dan, but Avi just calmly swiveled back and caught the ball.

"Are you guys okay over there?"

"Sure, Coach." Avi smiled.

Then the boys got back to work. Avi knew the sequence of pitches that Reuven liked to throw well enough so that they didn't even need to talk it over or exchange signals.

"Mark says the Dodgers are tough," Avi announced, once they had settled into their routine.

"Umm-mmm."

"He says they're one of the toughest in the league."

"Yeah, yeah. I heard him, too."

"He says he likes playing openers against a tough team because that's a great way to test your skills right away."

"Can't you just shut up?" Reuven growled. "I'm trying to concentrate."

Reuven didn't want to think about testing himself. He just wanted to get his kick right, his landing perfect, and remember to follow through.

When the game started, the Tigers took the field first. Reuven jogged out to the mound. Henry took his place at third, Dan at first, and Steve was in the outfield. While Reuven waited for Avi to strap on his shin guards, he took a moment to scan the bleachers. Dad nodded when he caught Reuven's eye. Mom stood up and waved. Reuven tried not to react in any way to that. She could be anyone's mom. No one had to know that she was waving at him.

There was a crater in the pitcher's mound where Reuven's left foot would land as he came forward on his pitch. All the mounds in the fields they'd used had craters from so many kids pitching in so many games. Dad often joked that when they got to the major leagues, they wouldn't know how to pitch without a gouged-out hole in the middle of the mound.

Major leagues. Dad was kidding, of course.

Reuven practiced his step a few times. He fit his right foot on the rubber and lunged forward, landing comfortably in the crater. Avi finally had all of his catcher's gear on and squatted in place.

Reuven's warm-up pitches were wild. After Avi had retrieved the third ball that soared over his head, he loped out to the mound.

"See the tall kid over there?"

"Huh?" Reuven snatched the ball out of Avi's outstretched hand. "What tall kid? The one taking practice swings?"

"Yeah. He's their leadoff batter. Dan knows him. Says he's good but swings at everything. Let's warm up on strikes. Then when he steps up, you throw outside. I'll bet we can fool him."

Reuven just stared at his brother.

"I'm the catcher. I'm supposed to come up with strategy." Avi laughed, then headed back to his position behind the plate.

Warm up on strikes. Like Reuven would purposely try to warm up on wild pitches. He threw a strike, concentrating on technique without trying for speed. Then he placed three more perfect strikes, each with just a little more on it.

The umpire called, "Balls in." Everyone got in position, and the Dodgers' hotshot batter stepped up to the plate.

"Okay, Reuven!" Avi called. "Let's do it."

"Yeah, Roo-Vane," the Dodgers' batter added, grinning out at Reuven. "Let's do it."

Reuven stared. That batter looked familiar. Was he one of Steve's friends from the library?

"Launch that ball in here, Roo-Vane. Steve says you're good, but I don't think so, Roo-Vane."

"All right, boys," the umpire spoke quietly. "Knock off the chatter, and let's play ball."

"Roo-Vane. Roo-Vane."

The Dodgers' bench had seized the chant and was singing with joyful voices. "Roo-Vane. Roo-Vane." They sounded like a field of mooing cows.

Reuven tried to concentrate. He thought about throwing his first pitch in a league game. He had dreamed a long time about this, and there had never been any mooing-rooing in his dreams.

Reuven tried to focus on his first pitch. He wanted more than anything to throw a blazing strike. He itched to burn this ball right by Steve's stupid friend.

But Avi's glove was hovering at the outside edge of the plate. Strategy. Avi had never even played catcher before. Now all of a sudden, he thought he knew about strategy.

The batter stepped in, focusing on Reuven. Avi slipped

his glove just a little more to the right, beyond the edge of the strike zone. Reuven fired to the glove. Not particularly fast or hard but straight to the glove.

"Stee-rike!" the umpire yelled as the batter swung wildly, trying to chase a ball outside of his reach.

"Roo-Vane. Roo-Vane."

The Dodgers' bench was still singing and laughing.

Reuven glanced up as if their noise wasn't bothering him a bit. He noticed his parents in the stands. Mom was standing up, and Dad was tugging on her hand, patting the seat next to him. It looked like they were arguing.

The one thing Reuven did not want right now was for his mom to make an issue of this. He could just imagine her stalking over to the Dodgers' coach, threatening to file some sort of formal complaint.

You've gotta keep her under control, Dad, Reuven thought. When he dared to look up again, he saw his mother sitting, staring off into the distance. She didn't look happy, but Reuven was relieved that she was back in her seat. He tried to ignore it all and just concentrate on his next pitch.

Avi's little bit of strategy had worked for the first pitch. He was set and waiting now with his glove in the exact same spot. Reuven stared in. Did Avi really think this guy was dumb enough to fall for the same trick twice?

Reuven stared and Avi held his glove steady. Fine. If Avi thought he was going to make up strategy, then Reuven would give him strategy. He fired to Avi's glove, outside the strike zone, just like before.

"Stee-rike!"

"Come on, Jack," one of the kids on the Dodgers' bench yelled. "He's throwing way outside. Stop swinging at the junk."

So, his name was Jack. Reuven felt certain, now, that this "Jack" was one of Steve's friends from the library. Maybe it was this Jack guy who had screamed out the car window and set the whole yeshiva making fun of him.

"Roo-Vane. Roo-Vane."

Avi set his glove, square in the middle of the strike zone.

Reuven had practiced pitching so much and had thought about it so often that sometimes it almost seemed like slow motion to him. He could picture in his mind the diagrams that he had studied over and over. The windup, the kick, the stride forward that ended in perfect position, and the follow-through. Always the follow-through. Dad had said that would make a huge difference in the power of the pitch.

Reuven almost believed, just for a moment, that he was practicing in the backyard. He concentrated on each facet of his movement. He relaxed and let all those hours of practice take over. The windup, the kick, the stride.

Jack's bat was cocked and ready. Avi waited.

The ball exploded out of Reuven's hand. He heard the pop of the ball smacking against Avi's glove just as he pulled out of his follow-through. He straightened up and looked in toward the plate.

Jack hadn't moved. Jack still stood, hunched slightly, with his bat cocked and ready—even now—even with the ball safely nestled in Avi's glove.

Strike three, and Reuven had struck out the first batter he'd ever pitched to in a league game.

"Yow! Not bad, Roo-Vane." Jack looked down at home plate and then back at Avi, who held his glove out to show off the ball before flashing a wide grin.

"Sit down, Jack. You're done." Steve's voice rang loud and clear all the way from the outfield.

Reuven felt a chill creeping through his body despite the sunny day. He looked around slowly wondering for a moment where he was. Was this a baseball diamond? Was this the first time he'd ever pitched in a league game? Had he really just struck out the first batter that he'd ever faced as a real pitcher, in a real league game, on a real baseball diamond?

"Shw-e-e-t-shwu"

Reuven swiveled toward Mark. Mark must want to send him a signal. This was no time to be thinking like this. This was a time to work. Reuven tried to clear his head and review in his mind the signals that Mark had taught them. But Mark didn't send any signals. He put his hand up to the bill of his cap and tipped it slightly toward Reuven. A baseball salute. Then he smiled.

Avi loped out to the mound once more.

"Got your first K," Avi said with a grin, because K was how you marked a strikeout on a baseball scorecard.

"Yeah, I guess," Reuven mumbled, and he couldn't help imagining a scorecard with his name as the pitcher and a great big K written for the first batter. "Your idea worked out pretty good." He took the ball from Avi and waited. "So what should we do with the next guy? What do you know about him?"

"Not a thing." Avi flashed a wink at his brother. "Don't know anything about anyone else. But I thought I'd come out here, anyway. To keep them guessing."

Reuven glanced over at the Dodgers' bench. They were all watching him and Avi. No mooing-rooing. Reuven nodded at Avi like they had just agreed on something, then Avi headed back to his position.

As Reuven waited for his brother to lope back to home plate, he took a moment to scan the crowd. Dad and Simcha were sharing a bag of popcorn. Mom waved and looked a lot happier now. Some of his other friends from school were there. Way at the end of the stands, Reuven caught sight of a girl with a head full of flouncy black curls.

It was Rachel Cohen. She was looking down writing something. Then she turned her face up and flashed a bright smile right at him. This time he was sure that smile was meant for him. Reuven wished he could smile back. But Avi was in place, and it was time to get back to business.

Reuven didn't need much more strategy after that first hitter. Mostly, he just threw as fast and as hard as he could.

Three innings. Five strikeouts. And the rest of the team was fielding so well that nobody on the Dodgers even reached first base.

The Dodgers' pitcher didn't have such an easy time of it. In the first two innings, he gave up four walks and two hits. Avi had one of the hits. A dribbler that could have been an out, but Avi always was lucky. Still, the Tigers had not managed to score and it was 0–0 coming into the bottom of the third. At bat this inning—Avi, Reuven, and Steve.

Avi swung at the first pitch. A lot of coaches told kids not to do that. They said it was better to look over the first pitch to get a feeling about what the pitcher is doing. How much stuff he still had. But Avi swung, smacking a bullet shot that skimmed past the second baseman and barreled into the outfield. He might have stretched it to a double, if the first-base coach hadn't signaled him to hold up.

Two for two. Reuven could feel that old, rumbling knot in his stomach. That jealous thing that he hated to feel and knew he shouldn't feel, but there it was. His little brother was two for two. And so far, Reuven was zero for one. He just had to do something this time up.

Reuven stepped into the batter's box. He set his feet, bounced his knees lightly a few times, and raised the bat to a comfortable position. He waited.

Reuven didn't move much in the batter's box. He didn't work the bat once he settled it in a comfortable position. He didn't bounce or jiggle his foot. He didn't swish the dirt around home plate. He got set, and he waited.

The sun was high in the sky, dropping a few shadows on the field. Sounds floated away. Voices from the stands fluttered by as indistinct as the flip of a bird's wing. Reuven watched and waited.

The first pitch was low, but not by a lot. Like most pitchers, Reuven knew the strike zone very well and saved himself for balls that stayed in that imaginary rectangular space required by the rules. He held his stance, did not turn around, and assumed the silence meant the umpire had raised his left hand to signal a ball.

The next pitch came fat and full through the middle of the strike zone. Reuven swung—just a little late. He knew he was late. He felt it. He caught the ball a little too far down the bat and sent it spearing high into the air. It would either be a foul, or the catcher could put him out.

The catcher flipped his mask to the ground and positioned himself. There was nothing more Reuven could do, so he just waited and watched.

"Foul ball! One and one," the umpire called as the ball dropped with a thud just behind the catcher.

Reuven stood in again. One and one. Two more chances to show the coach he could hit, too. Just like his little brother.

The next pitch was a loopy slow ball that Reuven should have knocked into the outfield. He didn't. He swung too soon this time. One and two.

Reuven waited. The next pitch was high. Way high. He

let it pass.

"Strike three!"

Strike three? That wasn't even close. Still, Reuven knew better than to argue with the umpire. That was the coach's job. He heard Mark screaming but didn't bother to listen to his words. It really didn't matter. Umpires never changed their minds, anyway.

Reuven dropped his bat and turned toward the bench. Mark was still screaming. But not at the umpire. Mark was screaming at him! His teammates were all pointing toward the Dodgers' catcher who was scrambling to retrieve the ball as it rolled toward the backstop. It was a dropped third strike, and you can run on a dropped third strike. Reuven spun around, saw that Avi was already sprinting toward second, and took off for first.

Voices erupted across the field. Where had they come from? Until now, Reuven had barely been aware of sounds from the crowd. He easily picked out his father's voice. "Run, Reuven!" And Simcha's voice, too, with that Russian accent.

Reuven had no idea where the ball was now. Had the catcher retrieved it yet? Was he just now ready to make the throw to the first baseman or was the ball already in the air, racing him to the base? He focused on reaching the base, stretching his legs as wide as he could before tightening his muscles to thrust himself forward.

First base was one step away. He burst across the bag running, still on his feet, just as he had been taught to do, and made sure—absolutely, positively, sure—that his foot scraped the bag. Reuven could not hear over the screams, and his back was to the umpire. He had no idea if he was safe or had been tossed out. When he finally slowed enough to look back, he saw the first-base coach smiling and clapping.

Safe. On a dropped third strike. That wouldn't count as a hit but at least he had a chance to score a run.

Steve came up next and hit a line drive double. Avi and Reuven both scored, putting the Tigers up 2–0. Two outs later, Henry blooped a single that brought Steve home. By the top of the fourth, the Tigers were up by three.

Reuven strolled out to the mound and began to lob in his warm-up pitches, nice and easy. His arm felt fine. The sunshine was bathing his shoulders and his back, soothing and relaxing his muscles. He felt loose and strong.

In this age group, games lasted seven innings and pitchers were not allowed to throw more than four innings. So, this would be Reuven's final inning as a pitcher in this game. It would be the end of his first pitching performance in a league game. He knew he hadn't shown much in the way of hitting yet, but he sure was pitching okay. So far, he was throwing a shutout—and more than that, a perfect game.

The first two outs came easily. One high pop-up that Avi snagged for an out and one more strikeout. That brought up Jack, the Dodgers' leadoff batter.

Jack grinned at Reuven but said nothing. No

mooing-rooing. The Dodgers' bench had dropped that chant. Reuven hadn't heard it since the first inning.

Jack settled into his stance, and Reuven stared hard at Avi. Avi shrugged very slightly and set his glove outside the strike zone. Why not? It had worked before. Reuven threw to the glove, but this time Jack let the ball sail by. Ball one.

"Hey, I'm not stupid, Roo-Vane. Gimme something to hit, or I'll just take a walk."

"Okay, boys," the umpire warned. "Let's just play ball."

Avi set his glove in the strike zone, and Reuven went with all the speed he could muster. Jack swung but couldn't quite catch up to the ball. Strike one. Then Avi shifted his glove toward the inside edge of the plate.

Reuven focused on Avi's mitt. If he missed, he could hit the batter. Reuven hated throwing to the inside. He didn't mind doing it in practice, but when there was a real live batter standing there, he always worried about hurting someone.

Reuven's throw was accurate, but he took a little off the speed, just in case. Jack tabbed the ball with a powerful swing that sent it soaring to the outfield. The left fielder took off running toward the foul line, then held up when he saw that the ball was arcing far to the left. Just a long, energy-wasting strike.

Reuven listened to the *thumpa-thumpa* of his heart. Could the people in the stands hear it?

One and two. One more strike and he could sit down

with a perfect performance. That ought to be something to remember when it came time for picking All-Stars.

Avi set his glove in the center of the strike zone. It was time for the heat. Reuven thought technique, technique, technique. Windup, kick, follow-through. This one needed to be perfect. Reuven reared back and gave it everything he had. He had never felt more powerful—more sure of his abilities. He thrust the ball forward with all the energy he could pull from his body, his mind, his will.

Jack connected square on and smacked the ball straight back—directly to Reuven—hurtling toward Reuven's face. There was one great simultaneous gasp from the spectators, as if they were an orchestra and the conductor had given them their cue.

Reuven whipped his arm up to ward off the ball. It glanced off his forearm, struck him square in the chest, then dropped with a thud at his feet.

Throbbing pain ripped through his arm, and every drop of air drained from his lungs. His brain told him to breathe, but the muscles of his chest refused to respond.

Reuven never liked to admit pain, but this was beyond him. He fell to his knees and hunched forward. After an eternity, his lungs came back to life, and he dragged in a great swallow of dust. The ball waited patiently between his knees.

Reuven looked to his side. He saw Jack racing for first base and Dan waiting with an outstretched glove for a throw that wasn't going to happen. But it had to happen.

He picked up the ball and chucked it toward Dan. Then Reuven grabbed his throbbing arm and collapsed onto his side.

It was not a good throw. It wasn't fast, and the ball bounced in front of Dan, making a short hop up to his glove. Not the sort of throw that Reuven would normally make, but it was good enough.

The instant the umpire called Jack out, Avi and Mark sprinted for the mound. Reuven was already struggling to his feet.

"I'm okay." Reuven groaned. "Did we get him?"

Reuven was still trying to get his breath back, and he leaned a bit on Avi as they made their way back to the bench. Mark insisted that Reuven sit out the next inning with an ice pack on his arm. In the final three innings, Reuven played outfield and no balls came his way. Avi took shortstop for the last three innings and played that position as well as he had caught.

This time Reuven didn't mind watching his brother do well. He felt good about his pitching performance. Now, he could sit back and enjoy watching Avi snag everything that came near him. Reuven even managed a hit in the last inning, ending up one for three on the day.

"Great job, Tigers!" The game had ended, and Mark gathered the team for a well-deserved rest and congratulations. "A 5–0 shutout for your opening game. That is something to be proud of, guys."

"We are good, man!" Steve screamed loudly enough to be sure the Dodgers' bench could hear. "We are great."

"Yes," Mark agreed. "You are good. But we have many more games to play. Enjoy this one. Then be ready to get down to work for the next game. Okay. A few comments. We're going to do lots of batting practice this week. We got a few breaks on the fielding today, but not every team is going to make those errors. Our bats were just a little too quiet."

Reuven wondered if those words were meant especially for him.

"But how about that pitching today?"

"Yeah, Reuven," several team members cheered.

"That was a superb performance, Reuven. And a gutsy one, too."

Reuven nodded without permitting himself to smile.

"And Avi, your catching was great today. You're tough, just like a catcher should be. I know you were hoping to pick someone off second, but you'll get a chance one of these days."

"Not bad at shortstop either," Reuven said quietly.

"That's right," Mark agreed. "Not at all bad at short-stop either."

Mark went on to single out other players for compli-ments, and Reuven cheered as loud as anyone. Then just before Mark dismissed the team, he added one more comment.

"I don't want to forget to mention that clever pitching

strategy. It really got us started out on the right foot. Good thinking from the Silver brothers."

Reuven and Avi took a few minutes to talk to their friends from school, then piled into the car with Mom and Dad. Before they could pull away, Rachel came by and walked right up to the open window next to Reuven.

"You sure were good, Reuven," she said in the most musical voice Reuven had ever heard. "Look." She held up a scorecard, which she had been filling in. Reuven was amazed. Most of his friends didn't know how to keep score. It never occurred to him that a girl would know how. But what amazed him most was all the Ks on the Tigers' side of the card. Every one of them was a strikeout for Reuven. It looked just as good as he had imagined it would. "Does your arm still hurt—where you got hit?" Rachel interrupted his thoughts.

"It'll be fine," Reuven stammered.

"You were good, too," she said, leaning down to see Avi. "Well, I've gotta go. Maybe, I'll see you in synagogue." She waved and left.

Avi gave Reuven a poke in the ribs and waggled his eyebrows. Reuven just shook his head, but Avi wouldn't give up.

"I think she likes you."

Reuven shushed his brother as he pointed toward their parents in the front seat, hoping that Avi would get the point.

"Don't you think she's cute?" Avi whispered. "Did you

notice she was even keeping score?"

"Will you shut up?" Reuven hissed.

"Boys!" Mom turned around "What's wrong?"

Reuven just shook his head and cradled his arm against his chest. No one said much after that. Dad and Mom kept glancing back with worried looks on their faces. They probably thought Reuven was so quiet because he was still hurting. He was still hurting a little, but mostly he was just thinking.

Rachel was cute. Really cute. But Reuven had more important things to worry about right now.

Avi's pitching strategy had helped a lot. And the coach liked it. Reuven needed tips like that for as many players in the league as possible.

As soon as they stepped in the house, Reuven headed up to his room. He dug through the drawers of his desk until he found what he was looking for. A small pocket-size notebook.

At the top of the first page, Reuven wrote "DODGERS." Then he listed the eleven players beginning with Jack. He couldn't remember everyone's name, so for those boys, he wrote a short description like: "thin, blond, glasses." He left a few lines below each name or description where he wrote whatever he could remember about that person's hitting. "Swings at outside pitches." "Power hitter to the left." "Sucker for low balls."

Then he went to find Avi. He showed him what he was doing, and Avi remembered things about some of the players that Reuven hadn't remembered. Between them, they were able to write down something about almost every player on the Dodgers.

After Avi went downstairs, Reuven flipped to the back of the notebook and wrote:

> Game 1—pitched four great innings
> fielded pretty good
> only got one hit

Not a bad beginning, Reuven thought.

His arm had stopped throbbing. He'd have a bruise, but it didn't seem to be swelling. It wasn't any worse than a lot of other injuries that he'd had.

Pitching today sure had been fun. Reuven plopped onto his bed and leaned back with his arms folded behind his head. Staring back at him from across the room was that great stack of history books and the pile of note cards that he had worked so hard on.

Reuven sighed.

He still didn't have a good idea for his history paper. But this was not the night to worry about it. Tonight, he just wanted to think about baseball—and pitching—and how good it had felt out there on the mound.

Okay. So there was one other thought that kept creeping into his head. And it had nothing to do with either baseball or term papers. That Rachel Cohen sure was cute.

7

Reuven watched Avi fiddle with his breakfast. He'd spent fifteen minutes getting just the right mixture of cereal, raisins, and nuts in his bowl. Now, he was stirring it more than eating it.

"What are you worried about?" Reuven asked, because watching his brother squirm wasn't really enough fun to fight off the boredom of the long day ahead of him.

"Nothing."

"You look worried," Reuven repeated, but he was crunching his own cereal at the same time, so it was easy for Avi to pretend not to understand him. And again after he swallowed, "You look worried."

"Shut up," Avi answered with a smile, then pushed his bowl away from him and went upstairs.

Reuven wished he had kept his mouth shut. He could hardly ask Avi to go outside and throw with him now.

School was out for the whole day for parent-teacher conferences, and his homework was done. Daytime television was boring, and he didn't feel like reading.

Reuven sighed loudly, even though there was no one downstairs to hear him. He went up to his own room, sighing loudly again as he walked by Avi's room. He got no response but left his door open, anyway, just in case. He took out the model airplane that he was in the middle of building and tried to concentrate. That didn't work, so he flipped through his notebook of baseball cards. That just made him wish even more that he was outside throwing instead of sitting in here.

He could straighten his desk. He pulled open his drawer and surveyed the neat line of pencils and pens, the paper clips in their box, the stack of notebook paper.

"Guess how many Ks."

"What?" Reuven looked up, happy to see Avi leaning against his doorframe. Although, of course, he wouldn't want to tell him that.

"Guess how many Ks you have. I just added them up."

"You did? Why?"

"Guess," Avi insisted.

Reuven didn't have to guess. "I have no idea." But, of course, he did know. Exactly. Six in the first game, four each for the second and third games, and five in last night's game. Nineteen. Nineteen strikeouts. He looked up at Avi and shrugged.

"Nineteen." Avi studied the scrap of paper he was

holding, ran his finger along the line of figures, nodded, looked up. "Yep. Nineteen."

"Yeah? Really?"

"Guess how many times I've picked a man off."

"Twice."

"That's right. How'd you know?"

"I just do." Reuven knew that and how many singles, doubles, triples, and walks for him and for Avi. He knew how many double plays he'd had. Well, just one, but that was a lot for four games, really.

"Do you think any other catchers have picked someone off yet?" Avi asked.

"Well, not that I know of. Mark keeps all the stats. He's got everything for the whole league. You could check with him next time."

"Really. I didn't know they kept stats."

Reuven wanted to ask Avi to check on ERAs and Ks for the other pitchers in the league, too, but he didn't say anything. Maybe Avi would just do it, anyway.

"I guess the Silver brothers aren't too bad then," Avi added.

"No, we're not. Not too bad." Reuven couldn't keep from smiling. "I wish I hit better, though."

"Yeah, me too." Avi wandered over to look out Reuven's window at their backyard. "We could ask Dad . . ."

"He'd never let us." Reuven interrupted, knowing exactly what Avi was thinking. Dad would never let them practice hitting in the backyard. Not since the second time they broke a window.

"Hey, you know what?" Avi said suddenly. "We could go to the batting cage. We could today because we don't have anything else to do."

"How would we get there? Dad's working."

But before Reuven could say any more, he heard a key in the door, followed by Mom's voice. "Hi! I'm back."

All of a sudden, Avi started acting fidgety again. He stuck his hands in his pockets and started jiggling one foot. It was the jiggle that was the surefire tip-off that Avi was nervous about something. That same trick would never work for Reuven. He jiggled constantly. Nervous. Not nervous. Busy. Not busy. Didn't matter.

"Hey, guys." Mom walked into Reuven's room and joined them by the window. "What are we looking at?"

"What did my teachers say?" Reuven asked even though he was pretty sure he already knew.

"Same as always, honey." Mom ruffled Reuven's hair a little. "You're doing fine. Everybody commented on how hard you work. No complaints."

Then there was quiet, and all three stared out the window for a few minutes. Or a few hours. It was hard to tell. Finally, Avi spoke.

"How about me? What did they say about me?"

Mom laughed. "I wondered when you would ask. Good reports on you, too." Avi sighed loudly. "What were you expecting? Mrs. Reynolds did mention that you were missing a few homeworks. But basically, everyone said you were doing fine. I was thinking that you and I could set up a system for me to check on your homework at night. Like we did last year."

"Oh, okay," Avi mumbled.

"So what are you guys looking at?" Mom asked again as she peered out the window.

"Nothing, exactly." Avi jumped in. "But do you think we could practice hitting in the backyard? Both of us have all our homework done."

"Glad to hear that. But didn't Dad tell you that he didn't want you hitting in the backyard anymore? You could play catch."

"But we need to practice our hitting," Avi whined.

"Sorry, honey. There just isn't enough room back there. We really don't want any more broken windows."

Mom started to walk out.

"Wait, Mom," Reuven said. "What about the batting cage. Could we go to the batting cage?"

"The batting cage?"

"We can pay ourselves. We both have enough allowance. Right, Avi?"

"Hmm." Mom looked like she was thinking it over. "I could take you, but I have errands. If I dropped you off, I couldn't be back until about two. That's too long, isn't it?"

"Oh, we don't mind?" Reuven looked at Avi, and Avi nodded as Reuven knew he would.

"But what would you do with the extra time?"

"They have miniature golf. We could do that."

"You have enough money for miniature golf, too?"

"Sure," Reuven said, but Avi didn't look like he was sure. "I can pay for Avi, too. I have enough." If he did that, Avi should pay him back, but they could talk about that later. Right now, he just wanted Mom to say yes.

"Well, okay. But hurry and get ready. We'll have to leave in about a half hour."

And both Reuven and Avi agreed because that was twenty-nine minutes more than they needed.

Avi had enough allowance for five tokens. Reuven bought himself ten and five for Avi. They got the same amount of allowance, and Reuven never could figure out why Avi always seemed shorter on money than him. But it wasn't worth arguing about today. If Avi got finished first, he'd just stand around and annoy Reuven, anyway.

They found two fast-pitch cages next to each other. Avi went into his, dropped in a token, and started slamming balls out to the long, green field before Reuven even had his batting glove on and his shoelaces double tied and his batting helmet set just right. He dropped in his first token, took up position, and waited.

The machine sits still at first, as if it's checking your token to be sure it's legitimate, then slowly starts to move. It's hard to tell what's moving, how you know it's moving, you just do. And the ball moves. You can see that. It sort of appears and rolls forward into position. The ball looks tan-colored or dirty. But that's just the shadows as it emerges from deep in the machine. Because all of a sudden, the ball is in place facing you, and then it's bright white. Like a star. Only it doesn't blink. It slings itself at you—suddenly—*boom!*

Reuven knew all this. Had seen it before. But it always took him by surprise, anyway. The white ball appeared, moving along like it hadn't a care in the world, until it flung itself at him. And Reuven drew back his bat and swung—thinking—level swing, level swing, level swing.

He connected. And there was that moment when the ball was pushing on his bat, trying to pull him backward, and he was pushing forward trying to force the ball forward. Reuven won as always. But only by a little. The contact wasn't solid, and the first ball shot forward, bounced against the backstop behind the machine, and rolled sideways, then drifted back until it was out of sight.

Foul ball. Probably. Or it would have been fielded, which is worse because then he might have been put out.

But the machine was already silently humming; another dirty, shadowy ball was rolling forward, turning bright sunny white before flinging itself at Reuven. So there was no time to think about the first ball, when the second ball was already coming at you. Reuven swung better this time and shot the second one out to the field where it landed in a garden of hard white balls, maybe next to one of Avi's, maybe next to a ball that had been hit by someone Reuven would never even know.

The first token bought him eight more pitches. By the time he had finished that set, Reuven felt like he was getting a better rhythm. He took a swig from his water bottle, readjusted his batting glove, dropped in the next token, and went to work again.

He only missed two balls completely. He tapped three others. The rest he hit solidly and enjoyed watching them fly out to land next to the other balls that had met their match in these cages. Some people thought working in the batting cages a bad idea. It wasn't the same as facing a real pitcher. The machine couldn't disguise the pitch that was coming or vary the speed or try some pitch that you didn't expect. Still, it was a good place to practice a level swing and concentrate on bat speed.

Reuven went through five tokens before he was ready for a break. Avi was already sitting on the bench outside the cages, munching on an apple. Reuven sat down next to him and reached into their snack bag, too.

"How are you doing?" Reuven asked as he slowly peeled a banana.

"Pretty good. I've been hitting them out pretty far."

"Yeah. Me too."

The curveball cage was right next to the cage that Avi had been using. A man who looked to be as old as Dad had just gone into it and dropped in his token. Reuven slid down the bench to position himself as squarely behind the man as he could. He watched the ball fly out of the pitching machine and tried to guess when it would drop. Reuven was surprised when it did, anyway. The man swung and missed.

He hit the next few, though. Reuven kept trying to guess when and where the ball would drop and was wrong every time.

Would his instincts know something that Reuven's head wasn't figuring out? Dad always said to relax and let your instincts take over. It worked a lot of the time. But Reuven wasn't sure just how well instinct was going to work if he had to face very many curveballs.

Both boys finished their snacks and got back into the cages. Reuven tried to approach work in the batting cage just like he would approach anything else. He would concentrate on one particular skill. The level swing. The speed of the swing. The follow-through.

As he worked, Reuven could feel a little irritation on his left pinky. For a right-handed batter, that finger took a lot of pressure. It was a spot where the bat rested and every swing pressed a little—on that exact spot.

Once a token was inserted into the pitching machine, ten balls were going to be flung at the batter. And this was the fast cage. It was not a good idea to turn your back on the pitching machine. Not even for a second because the machine's timing wasn't perfect.

Reuven's finger was really bothering him. But he refused to look at it. He concentrated on the balls coming at him and on his swing. When the set was finished, he took another break, plopping down on the bench.

He pulled off his batting glove and inspected his little finger. It was red, sensitive to touch, but there was no blister. He put his glove back on and looked closely at it, too. The spot right over that finger was worn thin. He tried to pull out the finger of the glove slightly so that the thin part would not be in that exact same place. He had four tokens left.

Reuven used two of them trying to ignore the soreness in that finger. By then, Avi was sitting on the bench gulping out of a water bottle. Reuven joined him.

"How many tokens do you have left?" Reuven pulled off his glove and inspected his finger again.

"I'm out. Did you get a blister?"

"I don't think so. Not yet." Reuven looked at his hand.

"Could come up later. That always happens to me. I hate getting blisters on my hand. At least it's not your pitching hand."

"You don't have any more tokens?"

Avi just shook his head.

Reuven didn't want to bat anymore. He didn't want a blister. It would be really stupid to interfere with his season because he got a blister working in the batting cage. He didn't want to waste the tokens either.

The boys just leaned back and watched people in the other cages. It wasn't a day off for the public schools so there weren't any other kids there. A few guys that looked like they could be in college, a few older men.

"You want to try the curveball cage?" Reuven asked.

"Me? I don't have any more tokens."

"We could split the last two."

"Yeah? Sure. I don't think I can hit anything, but it would be fun to try."

Reuven handed over one token; both boys put their batting helmets back on, and took over the two curveball cages. Avi hit one out of the ten. Reuven managed to tap one—barely. He came out of the cage shaking his head.

"They sure are hard to hit."

"Got that right," Avi agreed.

And Reuven couldn't help thinking how many more Ks he would have if he just knew how to throw a curveball.

The boys turned their bats and helmets back in at the desk and wandered outside. Reuven really didn't have enough money for both of them to play miniature golf, and he didn't feel in the mood for it, anyway. He did buy two Cokes, and he and Avi wandered outside to wait the hour until their mother would be back to get them.

They settled on a picnic bench near the miniature golf course and sipped their drinks. It was a beautiful spring day, wrapped in green and brushed by the lightest breeze.

"Nineteen Ks," Avi said as if they had been in the middle of a conversation. "Nineteen Ks for you and two pickoffs for me. Mmmm-mmmm-mmmm."

Reuven just nodded because there didn't seem to be much else to say. The numbers spoke for themselves.

"Not bad," a happy voice interrupted Reuven's daydreams. "Not a bad battery."

"Huh?" Avi sat up straight.

Reuven looked in the direction of the voice, then

blushed. "Hi, Rachel. Didn't see you."

"I heard you, Avi. I only saw one of your pickoffs. But I'm sure you're right. That's really great. You guys are good."

"You know what a battery is?"

"Pitcher and catcher. Everybody knows that."

"Yeah? Even girls?"

Rachel just rolled her eyes, and Reuven was glad he wasn't the one that had said that. Even though he'd been thinking exactly the same thing.

"What are you doing? What are all of you doing?" Reuven repeated when he realized that Rachel was there with three other girls.

"Well, um . . ." Rachel looked around her. Reuven looked, too, and realized that she was standing in the middle of a miniature golf course. Holding a little golf club. With a little white ball at her feet.

"Oh. I mean obviously. That was a stupid thing to say, wasn't it?"

Rachel laughed and nodded, but she could do that without seeming mean. She just seemed happy.

"Why don't you join us?"

"Can't. We don't have enough money. We just used it all at the batting cages."

"You don't have to pay, silly. Just walk around with us. They don't care."

"Are you sure?" Reuven looked up at the office like he'd been caught stealing something. "I don't think we're supposed to . . ."

But Avi had already stepped over the short fence that surrounded the course and was showing one of the other girls the proper way to stand—as if he knew. Dad had only taken them golfing—real golfing—once. Avi didn't know how to play golf any more than Reuven did, but there he was—offering advice.

"I just don't want to do anything that we shouldn't."

"You're so nice, Reuven." Rachel said, and Reuven wondered if she was teasing him—or if she thought he was being chicken or something. "Just walk around with us. If you don't actually play, I think it's all right."

So, Reuven did that. He stepped over the fence, too. But he wouldn't hold the club. He just walked with them as they moved past the windmill and the clown and came to one hole that had a sort of castle on it. He was just starting to have fun, when Avi grabbed his arm.

"It's Mom." Reuven looked up and saw that their car had just turned into the parking lot.

They both hurried off the golf course and out to the parking lot with just a quick good-bye to the girls.

Mom asked them about the batting cage, but she said nothing about the miniature golf course—or the girls. Reuven wasn't sure if she'd seen them or not. He wasn't even sure if they'd done anything wrong or if there was any reason not to talk about it. Still, he was glad that Mom hadn't said anything. He didn't know what he would say if she asked him about Rachel. All he knew was that it sure had been nice to see her and hear her voice.

A few weeks later, Reuven sat in his Jewish history class listening to Rabbi Schulman discuss Joseph—the Joseph in the Torah whose brothers had sold him into slavery. The rabbi was talking about how the brothers were jealous and all the bad things that come from jealousy. But, still, Reuven thought, Joseph had that great coat, and he was always dreaming about his brothers bowing down to him. You had to have a little sympathy for the brothers, didn't you?

What were you supposed to think, after all, if you had a brother who butted in every time you wanted to talk to your mom or dad? Or your parents got your brother a special coat and not you. Not that Avi had any fancy coats or anything—but he had other things.

And Dad knew it. That's why Dad would wink at the rabbi and say call on Avi. Avi can do it. Don't call on

Reuven. He'll just get all tied up and not say anything and embarrass everybody.

Reuven looked down at the empty sheet of paper in front of him and realized that he needed to be paying attention and taking notes. The rabbi had just started talking about that part where the brothers sell Joseph to strangers. Reuven wrote what the rabbi said, and he knew he was supposed to believe that the brothers had done a really bad thing. But think about it. What if you had a big family with lots of kids? You'd need money more than you needed one more kid, wouldn't you? You had to admit there was a certain amount of logic in that, even in a family with just two kids.

Focus, focus, focus, Reuven told himself. He realized he was daydreaming and missing things, and what if there was a pop quiz tomorrow? So he tried to concentrate. He tried not to think about Avi or even about baseball. But then the fresh smell of spring seeped in through the open window, and there was a hint of soft, new grass mixed in. Reuven could just about feel the dust wafting up as he scraped his cleats across the pitchers mound, and he could almost smell the leather of his glove.

A note plopped on his desk. He opened it slowly without making any noise and read, "Simcha said you mowed them down yesterday."

Reuven looked over at Peretz who sat across from him. He nodded, ever so slightly. Having Simcha at the Tigers' games had turned out to be a good thing, after all. He had come to all of them so far and was never shy about telling everyone in school about the games, always mentioning Reuven's best plays. Reuven kept meaning to tell Avi that he was glad he'd invited Simcha that time—for the first game—but somehow, Reuven never quite got the chance.

He kept his eyes on the rabbi while he reached down into his book bag and fished out a wad of paper about the size of a baseball. It had been worked through his fingers so much that it was hard packed and almost perfectly round.

He slid it down snug against the palm of his hand and only needed the quickest glance to get his fingers placed along the blue line that he had drawn around it to look like the seam of a baseball. He placed his first two fingers tight together parallel to the line on one side and his thumb parallel to the line on the other side. One more quick glance to check it out. Yep. Perfect grip for a curve.

Reuven could just see it—flying straight down the center of the strike zone. Then, *whoosh.* It suddenly dips, leaving the batter swinging at nothing but air.

Rabbi Schulman popped a question to Peretz. He did that sometimes when people's minds started to drift off. Reuven wasn't completely sure just what the rabbi had been saying, and from the way Peretz was stalling, it seemed that he wasn't quite sure either.

When Rabbi Schulman started bouncing questions around the room, you could never quite tell which way they would spring or exactly who would have to field them. Reuven usually enjoyed the challenge, but today he figured he'd be more likely to chalk up errors than to dazzle the rabbi with his agile thinking.

Reuven hunkered down over his desk. Every time the rabbi looked Reuven's way, he would hunch a little lower and concentrate on taking notes. He was very careful to avoid making eye contact, and he managed to get to the end of class without being called on.

Reuven met Simcha for lunch, as usual.

"When I can come to use your computer?" Simcha asked as he laid his sandwich on a napkin and carefully folded up its foil wrapping.

"You're finished with your paper already?"

"Except to type," Simcha said, nodding.

"Want these?" Reuven tossed a bag of chips across the table.

"You don't want?"

"Nah. I hate barbecue."

"Then why you bring?"

" 'Cause you like them." Reuven laughed while he pulled his own sandwich out of his lunch bag. "Come over Sunday after the game."

"How are you doing?" Simcha asked, as he crunched the chips.

"You ought to know," Reuven answered. "You're always there."

Simcha wrinkled his forehead and pulled his eyebrows together into a tight knot.

"Ahh," he said at last. "You think baseball. No. I mean on paper."

"Oh, that. I've got lots and lots of notes. I did my outline. The writing is going to be easy."

But Reuven knew the writing wasn't going to be easy until he thought of a good way to approach his subject. That's why he had put off writing for so long. He just couldn't seem to think of an interesting way to do it. What was wrong with just telling what happened at the Battle of Gettysburg? This happened and then this and then that. Isn't that how you were supposed to write history?

Both boys munched in silence until Avi wandered over and grabbed a chair at their table, without even being invited.

"I remembered something about that red-haired kid on the Yankees."

"Yeah? What'd you remember?"

"Well, for one thing, I remembered his name. It was Ted or Ed, not sure which. And he always swings early."

Reuven pulled his little notebook out of a pocket of his book bag. If it wasn't in his baseball bag or his book bag, then it was in a jacket pocket or the middle drawer of his desk at home. Anywhere Reuven went, the notebook stayed close by. He flipped it open to the Yankees' page and found the line for the mystery redhead. He wrote "Ted/Ed."

"I don't remember that he ALWAYS swung early. I know he popped up one of my pitches."

"It was one of your fastest pitches. I think you'd do better to pitch him slower."

"Says here he struck out twice, popped up once. How much better do I need to do?" Reuven snickered.

Avi just shrugged and chomped into an apple.

"You asked me what I remembered," he said, between loud, crunchy chews. "That's what I remember."

After Avi wandered back to join his own friends, Reuven started to tuck the book away and get back to his lunch.

"What is that book?" Simcha wanted to know.

"I keep notes about the players in our league. Then I can study them before we play a certain team and come up with a pitching strategy. My coach likes it."

"Can I see?" Simcha reached for the notebook.

"Sure. But it won't make much sense to you."

Reuven shoved the notebook across the table and went on with his lunch. Simcha carefully studied the Yankees' page, then flipped to the pages of a few other teams.

"Why you talk that way to Avi?" Simcha asked, still staring into the book.

"What do you mean? What way?"

"Mmm, short. Angry, I think. Like you don't want to talk to him. You don't talk that way to me."

"I don't talk any special way to Avi," Reuven answered. "He's just a kid brother, anyway."

"Oh." Simcha flipped a few more pages. "What kid brother mean?"

"Ah, you know, it's . . ." Reuven looked up and noticed that Simcha had flipped to the back pages of the notebook where all the personal stuff was written. He snatched the book out of Simcha's hands, tearing one page slightly.

"I'm sorry." Simcha diddled with his curly hair, the giveaway sign that he was rattled. "I thought you said I could . . ."

"Yeah. Yeah. It's okay." Now Reuven blushed a deep red. He knew he'd upset Simcha and felt bad about that. "I just needed to write something down while I was thinking about it."

Reuven flipped through the pages like he was looking for a particular spot. Simcha gathered up his things and left. As he slipped away from the cafeteria, Reuven noticed that he was still twiddling with his curls.

Reuven was going to pack up his things and leave, too, but the notebook flopped open to the partially torn page. He smoothed it down and inspected the damage. While he was looking, anyway, he read over what he had written there. He couldn't help himself.

"All-Star Prospects: 1-Avi, Steve, Me. 2-Henry. 3-Dan."

Reuven didn't really think Henry or Dan had much chance of being selected. But Steve's hitting had gone off the charts. His fielding still wasn't much, but he had two home runs. Hardly anybody hit home runs in this league, and Steve had two of them. Reuven had lost track of Steve's doubles and triples.

Reuven's hitting wasn't nearly as good, but he had gotten better since they started going to the batting cage more. Pitching and fielding were his specialties. Mostly pitching.

It wasn't Steve that bothered Reuven so much. He thought he had a good chance of beating out Steve for All-Stars. And if Steve got it . . . well . . . Steve was a heck of a hitter. He'd just go to the game and cheer for him.

Reuven wasn't all that worried about Steve.

It was Avi. Reuven's stomach felt like it was playing long toss with his just eaten lunch. Avi. His little brother. His kid brother. How did he get to be so good? How did he learn to catch so well?

Noise suddenly invaded the hall outside the cafeteria. Voices rumbled and ricocheted off the walls, lockers joined in with metallic clanking, and shoes kept time with interrupted, syncopated scuffles. Lunch hour was ending. The bell hadn't rung yet, but it would soon.

Reuven started to gather up his things, then just could not resist. He flipped the page and read some more. There were some notes he had taken after their game with the Cardinals. Mark had said something to another coach about Reuven's "shotgun" arm. The other coach had answered that it was a shame he didn't have a curve.

Reuven looked down his list of strikeouts. He had plenty of those, too. Lots of Ks. Why wasn't that enough to get picked for All-Stars. No matter what Reuven did, he always felt that he needed a little bit more. And he did need something more. An edge. A clincher. Something that would make Mark really notice him.

Today was Friday, and the yeshiva always let out a little early on Fridays so the boys could help at home getting ready for the Sabbath. Still, it felt like forever until the last class was over.

As soon as they did get home, Reuven asked Dad to help him with his pitching. But Mom said they needed to do some shopping and left Reuven and Avi with long lists of chores to get done.

"Avi, let's pitch a little," Reuven said shortly after his parents drove away.

"I'm not finished yet. Don't you have things to do, too?"

"Did them already. Can't you hurry? I want to pitch some."

Avi didn't hurry. It seemed like he worked extra slowly. Finally, he joined Reuven in the backyard with a ball and glove.

"Here." Reuven chucked the chest protector and shin guards toward him.

"I don't need all that, do I? We're just going to toss a little. Right?"

"Just put it on," Reuven insisted.

Avi got into his gear, then crouched in position. Reuven lobbed in a few easy pitches. Then he tried one. A curveball. He did everything just the way he'd read it in his pitching books, and sure enough, that ball curved.

After he threw it, Reuven swung his arm in a wide circle and flexed it at the elbow. Dad was wrong. Throwing a curve was okay. He felt fine. No pain. No discomfort.

He couldn't quite say the same for their backyard shed, though. The ball had veered so wildly to the left that it crashed into the shed, barely missing its small square window.

"What the heck was that?" Avi yelled over to him.

"That was my curve." Reuven laughed. "Needs a little work."

"You're not supposed to be throwing curves. Is that why you wanted to practice while Dad's gone?"

"I'm just trying it out is all." Reuven hated pleading with his brother. His little brother.

"But Dad said not to," Avi insisted.

"I know. I just wanted to try it. Let me do a couple more to see if I can get it over."

Reuven threw more than a couple. Some veered far to the left. Some dropped way in front of Avi, bouncing on the grass, then springing back up into his face. A few went straight across the plate without curving at all. Reuven tried out small adjustments after each pitch.

He threw a couple dozen pitches. Then he launched one that sailed in as if it was going to be an easy-over-the-middle strike. At the last second, it slipped sharply down sailing just a little to the left. Avi dropped his glove to meet the ball.

The boys stared at each other for a long, silent moment.

"Did you see that?" Reuven whispered.

"I saw it. I saw it," Avi answered in the same hushed tone. "That was a curve. That was a really great curve."

Avi stretched to his feet, tossed the ball back to Reuven, and hollered.

"WOWEE! A curve! I can't believe it. You threw a curve."

"I know. I know." Reuven stood riveted in place.

"Did you see what it did? It just . . ." Avi showed with his hand how the ball had come in and dropped and turned. "Like that. I could see the spin. Could you see it from there?"

"Yeah. I saw it. I'm not sure about the spin. I saw it drop. I looked up, and I saw it drop."

"Wow. Boy. That was something, wasn't it?" Avi hunkered down in his crouch again. "Bet you can't do another one?"

Reuven threw a dozen more wild ones before he got off another good one. An hour later, he was throwing one good one for every two wild ones.

"I think we should stop now, Reuven," Avi finally said. "What if Dad comes home?"

"But I'm fine," Reuven insisted. "I just want to get a few more."

They kept on working, but Avi popped up after every three or four pitches to steal a glance at the street.

"They're going to be back any minute, you know," Avi complained after a while.

"So what? When they show up, we'll stop."

"But what if you hurt yourself?"

"I'm fine, Avi. My arm feels fine."

"You sure?"

"I'm sure."

Avi got back in his crouch. After each pitch, he told Reuven what the ball had done, and Reuven kept trying out small changes in his motion. By the time Reuven heard his parents pull up in the driveway, he was definitely getting the hang of throwing the curve.

"So what do you think?" Reuven asked as he and Avi quickly stowed away the gear. "Should I try it Sunday?"

"I don't know." Avi shook his head. "I think by Sunday you'll be wild again. It took you an hour to settle it down."

"Yeah. I know. Let's practice it during the week. Then I can use it the next Sunday."

"Hey, guys," Mom called from the driveway. "Help me get the groceries in."

They hustled around to the front of the house, and each grabbed two bags out of the car.

The boys plopped the bags on the table, and Mom assigned them new tasks to do. Reuven hated being ordered around and particularly hated doing girl things like setting the table. But he knew better than to argue when Mom got into her Friday night flurry.

Then at dark, the Sabbath finally arrived and the house eased into calm. Everybody relaxed. The dinner was always delicious. Mom and Dad talked about vacations or relatives or politics but never about their work—or about schoolwork.

After dinner, Mom and Dad settled down in the living room. Dad had his newspaper, and Mom had a thick book. Avi and Reuven took over the dining room table to play games.

Tonight's game was Mancala. The players moved colored stones along spaces on a wood board, capturing stones as they went. The person with the most stones at the end was the winner. It was a simple game but with tricky strategy.

Reuven and Avi had a large collection of games to play on the Sabbath. Some were very complicated; others, like this one, were simple. But whatever they played, they played hard and they played to win.

Avi won the first three games. Then Reuven won a few games. Soon they were neck and neck. The dining room thundered and roared as each boy cheered his own victories.

"Are you two having a war in there?" Mom finally called out. "Can't I have a bit of quiet?"

"It is a war, Mom," Avi answered. "Brother against brother across the battlefield."

War. Brother against brother. Suddenly, Reuven's thoughts were racing. He forgot for a moment what he was doing, and in the next two moves, Avi had won. Reuven didn't even care. He didn't even throw anything at Avi for doing a victory dance around the table.

Reuven spent the rest of Friday night and Saturday thinking about brothers and the Battle of Gettysburg. He had read about things like that. There were families that were split like that during the Civil War.

What if one member of the family moved away. Like Mom and Aunt Sarah. They were sisters, but Aunt Sarah lived in California, all the way on the other side of the country.

So, what if there was a war, and it was the East Coast against the West Coast? What would Mom and Aunt Sarah do? They'd each agree with their own side. But they'd still be sisters. They'd still love each other and worry about each other. Wouldn't they?

That's what happened in the Civil War. Some families had people in the South and in the North. And there could have been two brothers—each fighting on the other side. They could even have met at the same battle, like at Gettysburg.

So that was a pretty good idea, Reuven thought. But he still didn't see how to tell it so it would be really interesting.

When sunset finally came and the Sabbath was over, Reuven hurried to his room and settled in front of his computer. He tapped lightly on the computer keys. He waggled his foot. He paced a couple of times across the room, then sat back down.

He wondered if it would be all right to talk to Mom. She always had good ideas. He wandered downstairs to find her, but she was talking on the phone. While he waited, Reuven flipped through the stack of mail lying on the kitchen counter. There was a letter from Aunt Sarah. Mom always passed Aunt Sarah's letters around for everyone to read, so Reuven didn't think she would mind if he took his turn now. He picked up the envelope, but before he could look inside, a thought struck him. It was such a good thought that he almost dropped the letter.

Reuven hurried back to his room. Now, he had an idea. A really good idea. A great idea, in fact. Mom and Aunt Sarah wrote to each other every week. That's what people did when they lived a long way from their families. Especially a long time ago when there weren't any phones or e-mail.

Soldiers always wrote home, didn't they? So what if there was a mother and she had one son on the Union side and one son on the Confederate side. They would write letters home. And she would care about both of them.

Reuven wanted to have each brother tell his story, day by day. But they would do it in letters home. Day one, day two, day three. Mr. Graham was going to love it.

First, there was rearranging to do. Reuven put the note cards for the Union side into three piles, one for each day of the battle. Then he did the same for note cards for the Confederate side. He reworked his outline, then discovered that the writing *did* come easily.

Actually, it was kind of exciting imagining what each brother would be experiencing and thinking as he wrote letters home. He wrote a brief introduction, but the rest of the paper was done as letters. It was different from a usual term paper, but Reuven liked it. He liked it a lot.

By the time Reuven finished typing up the first day's letters, his right arm was feeling a little stiff. Maybe a little sore, a little tingly.

He took a lemonade break. Then he settled back in front of his computer.

What if one of the brothers did something really heroic? What if he won an important medal? He'd certainly write home about that. Maybe the other brother, on the other side of the line, would hear about it.

Would he be really happy for him and send some sort of message over to tell his brother that he was proud of him? Even though they were enemies—sort of? What if it was the younger brother that got the medal? How would the older brother feel about that?

Reuven thought about that. He wasn't sure what kind of medals they gave during the Civil War. He decided to just stick to the facts. Probably, Mr. Graham would like that better.

It was almost midnight before Reuven finished writing up the second day of the battle. He was tired, and his right elbow ached. Pain sliced down toward his hand and crept up toward his shoulder. His fingers felt stiff and tingly.

Reuven changed for bed and did his nighttime prayers quickly. He kept flexing his elbow and working the fingers in his right hand to get his circulation going.

Probably it was from too much typing all at once. He had been so excited, though, and anxious to get his excitement down on paper. That had to be it. Too much typing.

He kept that thought in his head and locked out the other one. The one that kept drifting back to this morning when he had noticed a little pain. Maybe there was even a bit of a twinge Friday evening after he had spent two hours practicing his curveball with Avi.

The pitching couldn't have caused the problem. He thought of all the hours and hours that he and Avi and Dad had practiced baseball together. They'd often worked for more than two hours at a time. Of course, Reuven had never practiced pitching for two solid hours like that before. And people said you had to throw curves with just the right motion or . . .

Stop. That kind of thinking was silly. It was probably just the typing. It had to be the typing.

Reuven was sure he had nothing to worry about. By tomorrow morning, he was going to feel fine. He had a curveball now. Almost. Mark was going to love it.

Reuven knew he had a lot of strong baseball skills. Good fielding. Good fastball. He was starting to hit better. But it was like a jigsaw puzzle. You had to have all the pieces in place. And the curve. That was the last piece of the puzzle, Reuven thought. If he had that, he'd have a ticket to All-Stars for sure.

As for Honor Roll, Reuven thought his idea was going to make a very interesting term paper. Very different. Just the kind of thing that Mr. Graham would like.

Reuven settled into sleep, then woke again an hour later. His elbow throbbed now. It was far more than the dull ache he had felt earlier. The third time he woke in pain, Reuven decided to slip into the bathroom for a couple of aspirin.

Mom always liked to know when someone in the family didn't feel well. If Mom saw the aspirin bottle lying out the next day, she would want to know what was wrong and feel Reuven's forehead. He really didn't want to answer any questions right now, so he was careful to put the aspirin bottle back and rinse out the glass that he had used.

The aspirin worked. The pain slowly blurred, and as it did, Reuven's dreams focused on a perfect curveball. He could just see Jack hunched over the plate, smiling at him. Reuven drifted into sleep with the image of Jack's grin changing to shock as the ball dropped suddenly, leaving him swinging at empty air.

Yep. Curveball and a great term paper. This could turn out to be one outstanding year.

Avi was watching cartoons on television.

What a waste of a Sunday morning. Particularly since the Tigers had a game this afternoon.

Reuven sat in front of his computer trying to concentrate on the Battle of Gettysburg. He was still excited about the idea he had come up with last night—telling the story of the battle in letters—but it was hard to ignore the pain in his right elbow and even harder not to notice the dark clouds hovering outside.

The game wasn't until two o'clock. Reuven thought that would be plenty of time to finish his term paper. It would also give those clouds time to blow away and his elbow a chance to stop hurting. He wished he could take more aspirin, but didn't want Mom asking questions.

Reuven's keyboarding settled into a rhythmic *tap-tap-tap*. Mom was working in the kitchen adding the jingle of silverware and the clanking of china to the background noises. Avi's television program shrieked from time to time. Reuven was able to shut out all of that and focus on his work. He was even concentrating hard enough not to notice an undercurrent of deep bass rumbling that had joined in. Not at first, anyway.

"Reuven," Avi's voice interrupted him.

"What!"

"You don't have to yell." Avi walked over to Reuven's window and pushed the curtain aside. "Do you think they'll have the game? Look at it." He stood to the side and pointed out the window, as if Reuven couldn't see and hear for himself.

"That's just thunder. I don't see any rain."

"Sure looks likes it's going to, though. And they won't let us play if they see lightning either."

"I know. I know." Reuven glanced at his watch. It's only eleven o'clock. It'll probably . . ."

A loud crash of thunder ended Reuven's sentence for him and was quickly followed by the plop of large raindrops on his window.

"I just hate rain," Avi groaned. "Don't you, Reuven? We've already missed three games. I hate this."

"Yeah. Me too." Reuven joined Avi at the window. The sky was smothered behind a thick layer of black clouds, and the rain was starting to fill the air.

The boys stood together and watched for a while. Reuven wanted to get his paper done, just in case the game was still on. So he kicked Avi out and went to work. But the rain kept falling. And his elbow kept throbbing.

The phone rang downstairs. Then Dad yelled up to say that the game had been called. Avi groaned from across the hall. Reuven didn't want to admit it, but he was secretly glad. He didn't think that he'd have been able to pitch very well today, anyway, with his arm like this.

He finished his paper and went into the bathroom in search of aspirin.

"Hey, guys." Mom's voice startled him as he stepped out of the bathroom. He was so surprised that he gasped and almost dropped the two aspirins he was holding. Why did she have to sneak up on people like that?

"Sorry, honey. Didn't mean to startle you. But I was thinking. Mrs. Levine called yesterday. There's a Youth Group activity . . ."

"Mom, I hate those things."

"Just listen," Mom insisted. "They're visiting hospitals today. They have the sponsors, but they wanted a few more kids to go along. I thought you'd be playing today, so I said no. But since your game is off . . ."

"And I don't even know anybody that's going."

"Going to what?" Avi opened his door and leaned against it, swinging slightly back and forth. "What are we talking about?"

"Youth Group. Mrs. Levine was looking for people."

"Oh, yeah. I heard about it. Ben's going. You get service credits, too."

"That's right, Reuven." Mom nodded. "They give you community service credits, and you need them. You should go. You both miss so much playing baseball."

"Baseball's a lot more important, Mom. To us it is."

"Fine. But there's no game today, and this is just a couple of hours. You should do it."

Reuven knew when he'd lost an argument. So he just shrugged and agreed to go. Mom went downstairs, and Reuven ducked into his room to swallow his aspirins. Dry. He wished he could get a glass of water, but there was no point in risking having Mom see him. And want to know why. And then call Dad. And . . . and . . . and.

So, dry it was. And a Sunday to spend hanging around with sick people trying to think of something to say. Reuven would have much preferred to be playing base-ball. But then again—he did need the service credits. And his elbow *was* hurting.

A day of rest was probably a lucky thing for him. Three days really—because their next game wasn't until Tuesday after school. By then his elbow would feel fine and he might be able to try his curveball again—maybe just at practice. He could throw one during warm-up and act surprised—like how did that happen? And then the coach and Dad could help him get it perfect. Then he could throw it in the last few games of the season.

Reuven had never considered himself a lucky person. But all of a sudden—things did seem to be going his way. He wandered over to his computer and sent his term paper to the printer. He watched the sheets rolling out, one at a time. It looked good. Even just looking at it without reading, it looked good.

The rain was still coming down hard when Mom dropped them off in front of the girls' building. This was a mixed activity—boys and girls. The rabbis didn't really like having the boys involved in mixed activities—but the Youth Group activities were always well chaperoned, so it was allowed.

Reuven and Avi huddled near the door to stay dry. Mom had brought them early, as usual, and there were only a few other kids there so far. Avi's friend Ben arrived, and they went off in a corner to talk.

Reuven sighed. Who was he going to sit with on the bus if Avi stuck with Ben? Then, Simcha's dad drove up and let Simcha out.

"I did not know you come," Simcha said with a smile.

"I didn't know you were coming either," Reuven answered, relieved to have someone to hang with.

"I wasn't." Simcha reached for a stray curl hanging in front of his eyes. "I was going to your game."

"That's right! I forgot you'd have been there. I guess you figured out that there wouldn't be a game today." Reuven stuck his hand out to catch a splash of rain. "Not with all this."

"Well, your mother call my mother."

"Oh, I never even thought of that. Good for Mom."

"Mmm-hmm. And your mother tell my mother to do

this. I am needing credits for service."

"Yeah, me too. That's why I came."

"But should be good. Right? Good thing to do, yes?"

"Sure. Sure. Of course. I didn't mean—I just never know what to say to sick people."

"I think they give us magazines to give to them. If they like to read. And we say hello and hope you feel better. That's all."

"Yeah. I guess."

Reuven and Simcha watched the rain for a while as other kids started to arrive. There were a few other boys from their class. Lots of older kids who were close to graduation and probably needed to make sure they had enough service credits. But Reuven's eyes kept wandering back toward a small knot of girls who had arrived shortly after Simcha. And he particularly kept noticing Rachel Cohen. She had her back to Reuven, and every time she talked she moved her head just enough to send her mass of curls jiggling and swaying.

The sponsors arrived and organized everyone into groups. The boys would visit men patients, and the girls would visit women patients. Reuven, Simcha, Avi, and Ben were put in a group together, but when it was time to get on the bus, Simcha sat with one of his Russian friends, and Avi and Ben were together in the back. Reuven took a seat up front, leaned against the window, and thumbed through the magazine he'd been given to hand out at the hospital, as if he hardly even noticed that he was sitting alone. He hoped no one else would notice either. Especially Rachel.

Kids moved noisily up and down the aisle of the bus arguing about who would sit next to the window and if it was right to save seats or not. Reuven just focused on the magazine in front of him. He felt someone sit down in the seat next to him, but he didn't look up.

Then he heard the voice. That musical, laughing voice. And he felt the slightest tickling sensation against his right arm. It was not unlike the pins and needles that had been racing up and down his arm all day. Except this was a little lighter—a little more tickly—and not at all unpleasant.

Reuven glanced just slightly to his right to see the wisp of black curls brushing against him, and he froze in place. He couldn't even turn the page of his magazine. He didn't have the courage to move closer to the curls, and he certainly wasn't going to take the risk of moving out of their reach. So he stared intently at the car advertisement in front of him and sat as still as he could.

The bus finally lurched away from the curb and rumbled down the road. As the bus swayed from side to side, the curls moved—sometimes away and sometimes back—swishing against Reuven's arm with a feathery lightness.

"Hey, Reuven." That magical, musical voice. "Hey, Reuven."

And she waited, so he had to look up, had to smile and nod and say hey back, and wish he could think of something else to add to the "hey."

"Weren't you supposed to be playing baseball today? I usually go—but it rained—so I came here instead. Guess you did, too."

"Umm. Yeah. We got rained out. Well, I guess," Reuven looked at the sheets of water slithering down the window of the bus and felt so—so—stupid. "I guess you figured that out."

"Did you know I went to most of your games? Remember, I saw you at the first game. I didn't know if you saw me at the other games. My brother takes me. I love baseball. I can keep score better than my brother, too. He always gets mixed up on how to do it. You're really good. Everybody says so."

"They do?" Reuven tried to think who would have said that—or even thought that. "I mean who says . . ."

"Oh, everybody. My brother and his friends. My dad. And me. I think so, too. You don't mind me coming to your games, do you?"

"Sure. I mean no. I mean I don't mind. Anyone can come." But that sounded really bad, and it wasn't at all what Reuven wanted to say. "I mean, it's nice that you come."

Rachel laughed, and Reuven wondered if she was laughing at how dumb he sounded. But she looked happy and friendly so he hoped that wasn't it.

"What are you reading? They gave me this." Rachel held up a fishing magazine, and Reuven noticed for the first time that his magazine was all about cooking. "Isn't this silly. We're visiting women patients, and you're visiting men. We should trade magazines."

"Yeah. I guess they weren't paying attention." Any more than I was, Reuven thought as he passed his magazine to Rachel.

Then, Rachel talked and Reuven listened. He wasn't entirely sure what she was saying a lot of the time because it was so hard to concentrate on her words when her voice sounded so pretty. It didn't seem to matter, though. Rachel kept on talking, and every once in a while she asked Reuven a question. But never any hard ones, and finally she came back to talking about baseball.

"Do you like playing baseball?"

"Are you kidding? I love playing baseball."

"Even when it's hot?"

"Sure. Even when it's hot. I don't mind the heat. It loosens up my arm."

"What about when it's cold?"

"Oh, I don't mind that either. I hardly notice really. Although, it is harder to pitch when your hands get cold. But—I still love it."

"Are you the best on your team?"

"Well, I . . ."

"I think you are."

"You do? I don't know about that," Reuven said slowly.

"Do you want to be the best on your team?"

"Of course. That's a funny question." He turned a little

and looked squarely at Rachel for the first time. From up this close, anyway. "Of course, I do."

"But, see, I don't always want to be best. I play violin. I don't know if you knew that because we give concerts but only at the girls' school. But anyway, sometimes my teacher picks someone to play a solo. I don't want to be picked. I get too nervous. I want to be good. But I don't really want to be the best. Is it like that with baseball?"

"Not for me. Not at all. Absolutely not!" Reuven stopped for a moment, realizing how harsh he might have sounded. He worried that he might have upset Rachel or embarrassed her. He didn't mean to. He just got a little carried away. But she didn't seem upset. She was watching him and waiting for him to go on.

"I really do want to be best. I absolutely do want to be best. And the thing is," Reuven glanced behind him to make sure that Avi and Simcha were deep in their own conversations. Then he leaned a little closer to Rachel and dropped his voice a notch.

"The thing is the best person on the team gets picked for All-Stars. I really, really, really want to be picked for All-Stars."

"What happens if you get picked? Do you get an award or something?"

"There are trophies. But that's not the important part. The important part is getting to play in the All-Star game."

"So, wait a minute." Rachel held up her hand looking

just like a teacher trying to get the class quiet. "You're telling me"—and she paused, looked right into Reuven's eyes, before going on. "You're telling me that if you're really, really, really good—"

"The best," Reuven interrupted. "You have to be the best."

"If you're the best," Rachel said it slowly and carefully. "If you're the best, you get rewarded by playing MORE (*more?*) baseball. One more long, hot game of baseball. That's the prize?"

"Yep." Reuven smiled.

"That's it?"

"That's it."

Rachel laughed. She laughed that laugh that sounded like those tinkly bells that people hang on their porches. That laugh that made her look so happy—so pretty. And Reuven laughed along with her even though he wasn't entirely sure why it was funny. It just felt so good to laugh along with Rachel Cohen. He didn't even care that a sponsor looked right at them and wrinkled up her eyebrows.

"Okay, then. I hope you get it. I'm sure you'll get it."

"I don't know." Reuven turned serious. "I don't know. There are lots of good people on my team. And Avi and I have already missed three games because they were on Saturdays."

"But that's not your fault," Rachel protested. "They can't blame you for that."

"No. And the coach is great about it. But that just

means three less games for him to see what I can do. And then today didn't help because we could have been there today."

"The coach decides? About All-Stars?"

"Mmm-hmm."

"Well, I'm sure he'll pick you." Rachel clutched Reuven's arm, and he thought he'd never felt anything quite so cool or soft as her touch. "Even if you did miss Saturday games, your coach can still see how good you are. And when you do get picked, I'm going to come to the All-Star game to watch you." Rachel flashed her beautiful smile, and Reuven wished this bus ride would just go on forever.

But it didn't. A few minutes later, the bus pulled into the hospital parking lot and stopped. The sponsors quickly called out instructions, and people started filling the aisle and making their way off the bus. By the time Reuven got off, Rachel had already joined her assigned group and he needed to find his. There was barely time for them to exchange a smile and a wave before the sponsors led them off to make their visits.

The visits turned out to be easier than Reuven thought they would be. At first, he let Avi and Simcha and Ben do all the talking. But after awhile, Reuven found that he could ask some questions and offer a magazine. Some of the patients seemed glad to be able to talk, and all he had to do was listen and smile.

They were one of the last groups to finish, and a lot of

kids were on the bus already when they got back. Reuven searched the windows, spotted Rachel, and was relieved to see that she was sitting alone. He wanted so badly to sit with her on the way back. But could he do that? Just sit right down next to her like she had done on the way here?

Reuven paused for a moment as he stepped on the bus, hoping there would only be a few seats left so he'd be forced to sit with Rachel. But no such luck. There were plenty of seats left. He took one step forward. Just then, Rachel looked up, flashed a smile, and waved. She moved a sweater that was lying on the armrest next to her and pointed to the seat.

Reuven couldn't believe it. She wanted him to sit there. She had even saved the place for him. The aisle was filled with other kids moving very slowly. Reuven didn't think he could stand it as he slowly made his way back one row at a time. Just when he had two more rows to go, one of the sponsors came in through the back door of the bus. It was the gray-haired woman who had frowned at them on the way here. Kids moved out of her way, and it didn't take long for her to walk down the aisle and take the seat next to Rachel.

Reuven sat with Simcha. When they got back, most of the parents were already waiting. He was barely able to get a glimpse of Rachel as she hurried to hop into the car with her father. He watched them drive off without so much as a wave.

10

Mark always called for practices forty-five minutes before game times. Reuven and Avi often used the time to warm up while Mark threw batting practice to everyone else.

Avi was ready and waiting. Reuven was stalling. He dug through his bag for a batting glove, found one, put it on, took it off, then searched deeper in the bag for another one.

"You're using up all your time, Reuven. Don't you need to get warmed up?"

"I'm coming. I'm coming. This glove must have gotten wet. It's stiff."

"So what? You never use a batting glove when you pitch. What's up today, anyway?"

Reuven didn't answer. He didn't have to answer to his kid brother for anything.

Finally, there was nothing left to find in his bag, so

Reuven took his position facing Avi. He paused a moment to let the sun's warmth brush against his eyelids before pulling down his cap. Then, he wiggled his fingers to drive off the numbness gripping his right arm.

Avi tossed the ball, and Reuven raised his left arm to catch it. The ball skipped toward him as sunbeams sliced through the webbing of his uplifted glove etching shadowy bars across his face. It landed in his glove and, for a moment, nestled deep in the pocket.

Next, Reuven was supposed to bring his right arm up to snatch the ball and make the throw back to Avi. He knew how to do it. Dad had taught him to catch and throw a baseball more years ago than Reuven could remember. But today, he couldn't do it. His right arm hung at his side feeling like it was weighted with lead.

The ball waited a moment in Reuven's glove, then rolled out, plopped on the ground, and drifted lazily across the newly trimmed grass. Reuven grabbed his elbow, bent over at the waist, and tried desperately to smother the bolts of pain that were ripping through his right arm.

"What's wrong? Why did you drop that?" Avi jogged over to stand by his brother. Reuven turned away from him.

"Did too much typing over the weekend." Reuven moaned. "My arm's real sore."

"Typing? You mean when you did your term paper Sunday? You hurt yourself typing?"

"Well, I must have. I can hardly move my elbow."

"I don't think you can get hurt typing. Can you? You don't think it's because of what we did Friday?"

"No. It was the typing."

"Oh, man," Avi groaned. "I don't think you're right. I knew we shouldn't have tried a curve. Dad always said . . ." Avi shook his head and turned away from Reuven. "We are in so much trouble."

Reuven rubbed his elbow, trying to push away the pain. Of course, Avi was right. Reuven knew it. He had really thought that having a few days' rest would do the trick. But actually, his arm had been hurting more each day.

"It was my fault," Reuven admitted. "I'm not going to blame it on you."

"Big deal!" Avi threw his glove on the ground. "You can't learn to pitch by yourself. Everyone knows that. You don't think Dad will know that I helped?" Avi sat down on the ground, crossed his legs, and cradled his head in his hands. "We are in so-o-o much trouble."

"Yeah. I know. I'm sorry. I just wanted it so bad."

Avi looked up at his brother and shrugged his shoulders. "So what do we do?"

"I can't pitch."

"Not at all? Not even one or two innings?"

Reuven shook his head. "How am I going to pitch one inning? I can barely even move my arm." He went to find Mark, carefully holding his arm in the most comfortable position he could find. Mark didn't believe his story about the typing causing his problem. Dad didn't believe it either, and Mom rushed over to see what was happening when she saw Dad, Mark, and Reuven talking in a huddle.

Finally, Reuven broke down and admitted that he had tried to learn to pitch a curve.

"You did what?" Dad demanded.

Reuven explained that he just wanted to try it. Just a few times. But Mom kept wanting to know when and where and how. Then she and Dad looked at each other and thought for a while.

"When we were shopping?" Dad asked. Reuven nodded. "But we were gone almost three hours. You pitched for three hours?"

"More like two," Reuven said.

"That's right, Dad," Avi agreed. "Two hours. Maybe less. It wasn't three, was it Reuven? Couldn't have been that long."

Dad looked more sad than angry. Mark suggested that Reuven could watch the game from the bench as long as he kept ice on his elbow. Everyone on the team came over to ask how he was doing and tell them they were sorry he was hurt. But then they all sat as far away from him as they could.

Henry pitched the first four innings, giving up five runs. Mike pitched two innings and gave up four more runs. Avi pitched the final inning. He gave up one run, but the Tigers still managed to win 12–10.

The ride home was quiet. For once, Reuven didn't bother to take out his notebook and quiz Avi about everything he could remember about the other team's players. Simcha had been invited to come home with them for dinner so that he could stay to type his history paper on Reuven's computer. Even Dad and Simcha held the silence.

After they got home, Avi, Reuven, and Simcha settled silently in front of the television while Mom and Dad whispered in the kitchen. Finally over dinner, there was some conversation. Mostly about school and the weather. No one said much about baseball.

Simcha mentioned Honor Roll about a dozen times and was the only one at the table to ask about Reuven's arm. He said it sure was a shame and wondered if Reuven would be able to play next week. Mr. Silver changed the subject.

After dinner, Reuven gave Simcha a quick lesson in how to use the computer, then settled on his bed to work some math problems while Simcha typed. Reuven watched him slowly peck at the keys.

"Do you want me to type that for you?"

"I will do myself."

"It's gonna take forever."

Simcha twiddled his curls, thumbed through the pile of handwritten pages in front of him, sighed, and went back to typing. *Click. Click. Click.*

"Didn't you have a typewriter or a computer in Russia?"

"I don't know anybody with typewriter in Russia."

"Didn't you, at least, take typing in school?"

"We did not have in school either."

Reuven had to move to the dining room to work for a while. The slow *click-click-click* was just too annoying. He tried to concentrate on his math, but every wrong move of his arm set off sparking pains. And the pain kept jerking his thoughts back to baseball.

Finally, Reuven convinced Simcha that he had done enough of his own typing. After all, everybody here had computers in their homes and schools and had been typing since fourth or fifth grade. He promised Simcha that he would wait until his arm felt better, and if that didn't happen, he'd have Avi do it. There were only a couple of pages left to do, anyway. Simcha was reluctant, but he agreed and went home.

Reuven settled in front of the computer, jiggling his foot with the cadence of his typing. Typing did make his arm ache a little, but it wasn't so bad, and after a while the work became mechanical. His mind wandered off to more interesting things.

Reuven tried to believe that the pain in his elbow was a little better now. And there wasn't another game until next Sunday. Surely, his arm would be better by then. He wouldn't even think of trying a curveball next week, but surely, he would be ready to pitch by then. His fastball should be as fast as ever.

There would be two more games after next week's to

show off his curveball. In a way, that was better, lucky even. He would only use it a few times. That way it would be fresh in the minds of the coaches when it came time to pick All-Stars.

Reuven finished typing Simcha's paper, then ran it off on his printer so that Simcha could mark any corrections. He was tired. He lay down on his bed and quickly fell asleep.

Reuven's arm did improve considerably during the week. He was much better by Sunday's game, although not completely free of pain. Mark refused to let him play.

"Bring me a note from your doctor, if you want to play in the last couple of games," Mark insisted.

So Mom took him to the doctor on Monday after school. The doctor reassured her that Reuven would be just fine. He didn't expect any long-term problems.

"But will I be able to get—you know—completely back to normal?" Reuven asked. "Will I be able to pitch like before?"

"I don't see any reason why not," the doctor answered, and Reuven was so relieved he could hardly breathe.

The doctor took out his prescription pad, scribbled across it in that doctor-writing that no one can ever read, tore off the sheet, handed it to Mrs. Silver, then patted Reuven on the shoulder before leaving the room.

"See. I knew it wasn't that bad," Reuven said as he buttoned his shirt. But then he noticed the look on Mom's face.

She shook her head and silently handed Reuven the doctor's note.

Total rest—right arm—one week. No stressful activity—two weeks. Light activity to build strength—two weeks.

"But—this isn't right. I already rested it. I already did light activity. I already . . ."

"No, Reuven."

"But, Mom!"

"No, Reuven. We follow the instructions. That's it. Not another word."

She tucked the note into her purse, opened the door of the exam room, and walked out. Reuven stared straight ahead of him for the entire ride home. He stared so hard that everything blurred. When they pulled up at the house, Reuven jumped out of the car, hustled to his room, and slammed the door behind him.

He wanted to pull out a calendar and the Tigers' schedule to count off the weeks. But he didn't need to do that. He had the schedule memorized. There were two weeks left in the season. Two weeks. That was it. And one of those weeks, he was supposed to rest his arm completely. Then the last week, he was supposed to do only light activity. And no one—no one was going to call pitching light activity. Reuven couldn't even imagine anything that he could possibly say to convince Mark or Dad that pitching was light activity. And Mom. Mom would think yawning was too strenuous.

So that was it. Reuven couldn't even believe what was

going through his own mind. That was it. The end. The end of the season. No more pitching.

"Hey, Reuven." Avi tapped at his door. "So, is everything okay? You okay for the game Thursday."

"Get out!"

"What?"

"Get out!"

"What's wrong? Why are you screaming at me?" But Avi backed out of the room, anyway. "Man, you are one strange person."

Reuven didn't want to talk to anyone. Not now. Not ever. Except when Dad tapped on his door a little later and called to him, Reuven was relieved not to be alone with his thoughts anymore.

"I'm sorry, son. Mom told me. It's a tough break."

Reuven waited for the lecture. The speech about how it was his own fault. And what about, Avi? Was Dad going to understand that it was Avi's fault, too? Because it was, wasn't it? He could have stopped me, Reuven thought. He could have refused to keep catching for me. He didn't have to give in, did he? But Dad didn't say anything like that. He didn't even mention "fault."

"Follow the doctor's orders. And I mean to the letter, Reuven. I know you're disappointed. But there will be other seasons—as long as we do what the doctor says. This is bad enough. We don't want you getting injured in a way that could be permanent."

Dad patted Reuven on the shoulder, just like the doctor

had done, and left him alone.

Other seasons. Reuven began every season filled with hopes and fears. And this time—this time—for the first time Reuven could remember—it had seemed that the hopes were way ahead of the fears. Would that every happen again? Ever?

"Reuven?" Avi peeked in his door. "Now don't go and get mad at me, again. Dad just told me. I feel horrible."

"*You* feel horrible."

"I should never have let you do that. Shouldn't have let you talk me into it."

"I didn't have to talk that hard, you know."

"I know," Avi moaned. "It's my fault, too."

"Yeah, I know."

"I wish Dad would yell at us."

"Yeah, me too."

"I wish Mom wouldn't yell at us."

"Mom didn't yell at us. Did she?"

"She yelled at me," Avi said.

Reuven laughed. He didn't feel like laughing, but that was just a little funny.

"But, Reuven, All-Stars isn't until next month. That's five weeks before they even start practices. Look I figured it out."

Reuven sat up on his bed. "What are you talking about? Are you talking about me? You don't think they'd let me . . ."

"Why not? If you do what the doctor said, there's still

time for us to start practicing together a couple of weeks before All-Stars. You can get your strength back in a couple of weeks."

"I could. I know I could. But I just don't think . . . we'd work with Dad, this time."

"Absolutely."

"We'd do this the right way."

"Absolutely."

"And no curves."

"Really? I mean . . ."

"Avi! Shut up about that. I mean I'd be lucky if they just even let me be in All-Stars."

"Yeah, okay. I guess you're right. I just really wanted to see you throw one in All-Stars. Wouldn't that have been great?"

But Reuven couldn't think about throwing a curve in All-Stars. He could barely even think about being in All-Stars. It wasn't like it was any kind of sure thing before he got hurt. And this—this idea of Avi's. It was a long shot. Such a long shot.

Still, Reuven could see it already. He could feel it already. Standing on that mound. The loudspeakers. The crowd. Facing the best players in the league.

And it was possible. Possible. Just maybe.

It could still happen. Couldn't it?

11

The Tigers split their last two games, ending up 14–4. That was a first-place finish, meaning that the team would receive a trophy at the Awards Night. Mark gathered the team, one last time, to congratulate each player.

"Reuven, you've been a pleasure to work with," Mark said. "You're talented. You're dedicated. And you're smart. I don't think I've ever worked with a better pitcher."

Mark shook Reuven's hand. Man to man.

Reuven grasped Mark with a firm grip and shook confidently. Reuven wanted Mark to know that he was completely recovered. Just in case Mark was still thinking about picking him for All-Stars. He couldn't bring himself to say anything, so he just shook Mark's hand as firmly as he could, smiled, and hoped.

The next morning, Reuven and Dad were ready for the ride to school. As usual, Avi was still doing last-minute homework.

The history papers were due today, and Reuven had Simcha's as well as his own. Simcha had sent back some last-minute changes to be typed, and he had reminded Reuven over and over again to bring the paper to school today. Then he'd called last night to remind him once more.

Of course, Reuven never forgot anything. Everybody at school knew that. Under any other circumstances, Reuven would have been thoroughly insulted by all of Simcha's reminders, but this time, he was willing to take it in stride. Turning these papers in even one day late would mean that a B was the best grade you could get, and there would be no chance for Honor Roll.

"If I will make Honor Roll in America, my cousins will go crazy," Simcha had told Reuven at least one hundred times.

His grammar needed work, but the message was clear. Reuven wanted Honor Roll, too. And his paper had turned out very well, if he did say so himself.

Reuven began reading Simcha's paper. Even though he had typed the end of it and made many corrections, he'd never really bothered to read it all the way through. It was surprisingly good.

"We might as well wait in the car," Dad interrupted his thoughts.

Reuven grabbed his book bag and lunch and headed for the car, reading as he went. They were halfway to school before he finished.

"I don't see how he can do it," Reuven said when he finally looked up.

"Do what?"

"Write so well when he hardly even knew English two years ago."

"Oh, you mean Simcha," Dad answered. "He's a smart boy. And a nice one. I'm glad you're friends with him."

"Are those your Honor Roll papers or something?" Avi asked from the backseat.

"They're just term papers for history," Reuven corrected him. "But we have to get an A on the paper to have a chance for Honor Roll."

"And Simcha said it can't be late?"

"Right. It can't be late. Mr. Graham makes a big deal about that. You better hope you don't get him next year."

Dad pulled up in front of the school, and the boys scrambled out of the car. Reuven slung his book bag over his shoulder, then suddenly froze.

"Wait, Dad." Reuven's voice had twisted itself into a tight knot. He dropped his bag on the sidewalk, ruffled around in it for a moment, looked in the car where he had been sitting, then back down into his bag again.

"What's wrong, son?"

"I think I forgot something."

"I really have to hustle this morning, Reuven. I have a meeting. Can you do without it, today?"

"Yeah. Sure. I guess so." He slammed the door and

watched Dad drive away.

Reuven looked at Simcha's history paper that he was holding in his hand. His book bag had the usual collection of books, binders, and papers. What it didn't have was his own history paper.

He remembered having both papers, his and Simcha's, on the dining room table. He could see the two folders sitting together, one on top of the other, just as plainly as if he could reach out and pick them up right now. Then, he remembered, he started reading Simcha's paper and then Dad suggested that they wait for Avi in the car.

After that, Reuven's memory was a jumble. He walked out to the car. He obviously remembered to bring his book bag and his lunch bag because there they were, resting patiently on the sidewalk at his feet. It was that new blue binder with his history paper that had somehow vanished. Like magic. Terrible, wrong magic. It was not in his hands, not in his book bag, and not in his memory.

The dining room was the only place it could be. The blue binder, with the paper that would surely have been an A but now was going to be a B, must still be waiting for him on their dining room table.

"What's the matter, Reuven?"

Reuven ignored his brother. He headed for his locker where Simcha was pacing back and forth. As soon as Simcha spotted him, he rushed over, grabbed the report out of Reuven's hands, and began flipping through the pages.

Reuven shivered. His mouth was so dry he could hardly swallow. He jerked the door of his locker hard enough to set the whole row of lockers chattering. That's when Reuven noticed that Avi was still tagging along behind him.

"Don't you have your own friends to hang out with?" Reuven screamed as he spun around to face his brother.

"Thought you might need this." Avi held out the new blue binder with the report that would have been a B but now, thanks to Avi, had an awfully good chance of being an A after all. "You left it in the house and well, since I know you never forget anything, . . ."

Reuven was so surprised, he couldn't move. His friend, Peretz, rushed by on his way to class, bumped Reuven, and almost knocked him off his feet.

"I . . . I . . ." Reuven took the folder from Avi, opened it, and checked to see that it really was his history paper inside. "I mean, thanks. I didn't realize . . ."

"Yeah. It's okay." Avi hurried off to his own locker as if it was nothing.

Reuven watched him go and shook his head. It sure was hard to figure out kid brothers. Just when you started to wonder why anybody would want to have one, they'd go and do something like this.

Sunday afternoon seemed strange with no baseball game. Reuven wandered around the house, wondering what to do with himself.

It had been a whole week since their baseball season

ended, and there were two more weeks before the All-Star game.

Avi and Reuven had been playing long toss, and Reuven's arm was feeling fine. Dad had called the doctor, and they both agreed that Reuven could actually start pitching again tomorrow. As long as he built up slowly and quit at the first sign of pain.

Mark hadn't said exactly when he would announce his choice. He hadn't said much of anything about All-Stars at their final meeting, but it had to be soon. They would need at least a week to get the uniforms distributed and make plans for practices and the big game.

The phone rang. Reuven held his breath.

"For you, Reuven. It's Simcha," Mrs. Silver called out.

"Hi, Simcha—Yeah, I made Honor Roll. Mr. Graham told me at school Friday—He didn't?—But I'm sure you will. Your paper was great—Okay—Let me know— See ya."

"Did he make Honor Roll?" Avi wanted to know.

"You shouldn't be listening to other people's phone calls."

"Wasn't listening. You just talk loud. Anyway, I thought it might be Mark."

Now, why would Avi say something like that? Why should he be thinking about Mark and All-Stars? Reuven decided to steer the conversation in a better direction.

"Simcha left school early on Friday before Mr. Graham told everybody who made Honor Roll. He's still waiting to hear."

"Reuven." Mom poked her head out of the kitchen. "Did I hear you say something about Honor Roll?"

Reuven just nodded.

"Did you make it?"

Reuven nodded again.

"And you didn't tell us?" Mom planted her hands on her hips and stared at Reuven. "I can't believe you didn't tell us?"

"I guess I forgot."

"Oh, Reuven. You worry so much about baseball. Everything else just gets lost." She came over and planted a kiss on top of Reuven's head. "Well, I'm very, very proud of you. I'm going to go tell Dad."

She headed upstairs, and Avi made a kissy sound. So Reuven chased him outside, and they ended up playing catch.

"Aren't you glad you made Honor Roll?" Avi asked as the ball flew back and forth between them.

"Sure."

"You don't seem very excited about it."

"I am. I guess. I sort of expected it."

"Yeah? I wish I could expect things like that."

The boys were throwing nice and easy. This was just long toss. No pitching. That would be tomorrow. But then long toss was about the best thing Reuven could imagine doing when he needed to relax and think.

"You just need to work a little harder," he finally

answered Avi. "If you weren't always doing your homework at the last minute . . ."

"But I do it. What difference does it make when?"

"Well, I guess you'd do it better if you weren't always
rushed."

Avi sent the next throw at Reuven with some extra zip.
"Anyway, I expect you're glad now that I brought your
paper to you that day you forgot it."

Reuven was glad, but Avi had already turned and was
stalking back into the house. He couldn't play catch by
himself, so Reuven went in, too, and plopped down on
the sofa next to Avi.

"You thought that was Mark, didn't you?"

"What? When?"

"When?" Avi shook his head. "When the phone rang.
You thought that was Mark."

"No, I didn't."

"Yes, you did. And I did, too. I'm sure you're going to
make All-Stars."

"Ahh. No, I'm not." But Reuven thought—yes—
please, yes. "The thing with my arm and not playing in
those last games. I don't think I have much of a chance."

"Yeah. I know," Avi agreed. "But before that, you were
doing so great. Everyone was sure you'd get it."

"Everyone?"

"You know. Steve. Henry. Everyone."

"Really?"

"Sure."

"Henry and Steve are really good," Reuven argued. "Either one of them could get it."

"You're better, though."

"And there's you," Reuven said with a slight laugh. Avi making All-Stars. That was the one thought Reuven worked very hard to keep out of his head. "You're a really good catcher. And nobody ever wants to catch."

"But I'm a rookie. You said . . ."

"I know. They don't usually pick rookies. But next year . . ."

"Yeah. I really hope I get All-Stars next year. Hey, you know what Dan told me?"

Reuven shrugged.

"He said they sometimes pick a kid as an honorary coach. Would they pick a rookie for that?"

"Maybe," Reuven agreed. He didn't want to tell Avi that being a coach wouldn't be anything like playing in an All-Star game. Who ever dreamed of being a coach? You dreamed of making a great pitch or of sliding into home. But if it made Avi happy to think he might get to the All-Star game as an honorary coach—well, why burst his bubble?

Reuven was starting to feel a little better now. Avi didn't think Steve or Henry were good enough for All-Stars. And Avi was just a rookie. "But still, there's the problem with my arm."

"You're fine now," Avi insisted. "Your arm's better. Mark knows that."

"Really?" Reuven asked. "How do you know he knows?"

"Because I told him." It was Dad, who had just come down the stairs. "He called me a few days ago. He was concerned about you. I told him you were already playing some catch, and the doctor said you could begin working on pitching this week. He knows. And, Reuven, congratulations on Honor Roll. You should have told us." Dad came over and shook Reuven's hand. He did that sometimes, and it always made Reuven feel so grown up.

He wanted to ask Dad exactly what Mark had said when Dad told him about his arm. He wanted to know every word and how his voice sounded and all of that. But Dad was talking about going out to dinner next week to celebrate about Honor Roll, and it didn't seem like the right time to ask about Mark or his chances for All-Stars.

The phone rang three more times that afternoon. Twice for Dad and once for Mom. None of the calls were from Mark. They ate dinner, and Avi and Reuven settled in front of television.

The phone rang, and Mr. Silver picked up.

"For you, Reuven," he called.

YES! Reuven didn't trust himself to ask if it was Mark. He was afraid that his voice might waver or squeak. Avi watched Reuven walk toward the kitchen.

"Hello," Reuven said slowly into the phone. "Oh, hi, Simcha—Hey, that's great—He said that?—Yeah. It's really great—When are you telling your cousins?—I bet they did—Okay, see you tomorrow."

"Simcha got Honor Roll, too," Reuven explained as he hung up. His parents were very pleased, and they pointed out that it had been awfully nice of Reuven to help Simcha with typing his paper. Of course, Reuven mumbled that it was all Simcha's work, but really he did feel like he had done a lot to help. He was a bit proud of that if anyone wanted to know, but he wasn't going to say it out loud.

Reuven settled back in the living room, waiting for the phone to ring again. It didn't. The phone seemed to think it had delivered enough good news for one evening, and it remained resolutely silent.

Finally, the boys went up to bed. It was, after all, a school day tomorrow.

Avi and Reuven were thumping around in their rooms when the phone rang again. They both stepped out into the hallway and listened silently as Mr. Silver answered.

"Hello—Fine. How are you?—Oh, how nice—That's wonderful news—He'll be so excited—Yes, I have a pen—Uh-huh. Okay—Really!—That's a great idea. Thanks so much for calling."

Mr. Silver hung up, then stepped into the hall. Reuven and Avi leaned over the banister to see their father.

"That was Mark," Dad called up to the boys. "Congratulations, Avi. You're an All-Star."

12

Reuven filled in the entry on his scorecard to show the final out of the third inning. The second baseman for the Blues had popped the ball up for that final out. Still, the team had managed to bring one runner in to score so the Reds and the Blues were tied again.

Reuven marked the run and noticed how tightly matched the teams were. The first inning had ended 1–1. The second inning 3–3. And now, they were 4–4.

He flipped his card over to the Reds' side to get ready for the top of the fourth. Just as he did, a great drop of rain plopped down right on top of the line for the shortstop. Reuven wiped it away while a second drop landed on the back of his hand. Then came a third and a fourth.

"Toss those bats in, and everybody head for shelter," one of the coaches screamed.

Reuven tucked the scorecard under his arm and hurried

behind the stands to wait out the rain.

They would have called any other game. Not this one. This was the All-Star game.

The coaches decided to wait for the cloudburst to pass. When the rain stopped, Reuven went back to the bench and the coaches got busy spreading sand and kitty litter over the puddles that spotted the field. Two coaches and three fathers busily worked on the pitcher's mound, even though it was better right now than any dry mound Reuven had ever worked from. It didn't even have a crater.

The players waited in small groups or mingled with their families and friends in the stands. Avi leaned against the fence talking to Simcha and Dad. Reuven was the only person sitting hunched on the bench.

He was a coach, and he was not a coach. Mark had volunteered him as an honorary coach. Reuven supposed it was a consolation prize for not making All-Stars.

Reuven wanted to decline the honor, but Dad made such a big deal about it. So, he went along. Which was a good way to say it, because all Reuven did was go along— to the practices and to the meetings. He didn't have any real responsibilities, and everyone knew he didn't really belong there.

Jack wandered over and plopped down next to Reuven. They had played against each other many times since that first game that now seemed so long ago. Reuven and Jack had not exactly developed a friendship, but they had, at least, found a mutual respect for each other's skills.

"I wish they'd picked you for our team."

"Then I'd be playing against my brother," Reuven pointed out.

"What's bad about that?"

Reuven just shrugged.

"Sure is too bad about your shoulder."

"Elbow. And it's fine. My coach just thought . . ."

Reuven didn't want to think about what anyone else thought. Avi was in the All-Star uniform, and he wasn't. Those were the facts.

Jack walked away, and Reuven saw Rachel Cohen walking toward him. She was the last person he wanted to see today. But Rachel didn't seem to know that because she was waving and showing off that wonderful smile.

"Hi, Reuven," Rachel called out.

"Did you come to watch Avi?" Reuven asked without smiling back.

"I came because I like baseball, Reuven. And it's good to see you both. Is it fun being a coach?"

"I'd rather be playing."

"Really? But isn't being a coach better than being a player? Aren't you sort of a boss?"

No, Reuven thought. Being a coach isn't better than being a player. Nothing is better than playing. That's what he wanted to say, but Rachel's brother was calling her and Reuven found himself concentrating for a moment on the smooth, swingy way that Rachel walked as she headed for the stands.

Reuven shook his head. How could girls look so good and understand so little?

The coaches finished repairing the field. Its wet grass glistened below a sky that smelled of mud and honeysuckle. Reuven thought he would have loved to be playing baseball on a day like this—or to tell the truth, on just about any kind of day at all.

Avi strapped on his shin guards, then tied the chest protector over his blue jersey. His team was the Blues. Jack's team was the Reds, and they were coming up to bat.

The Blues' coaches were in a huddle with their starting pitcher, and they motioned for Reuven to join them.

"Reuven, we're trying to decide if Paul should keep pitching. He's allowed to pitch one more inning, but he says his arm is starting to stiffen up."

Reuven just shrugged.

"Our second pitcher got sick, so we're thinking to put in Roy. The thing is Roy's never pitched more than two innings in a game before. We could try to stretch him to three. But we'll have a problem for the last inning."

The two coaches turned to Reuven and waited. Reuven flexed his right arm, bending and stretching the elbow. That had become a habit with him. He looked at Paul. He was flexing his elbow, too.

"I guess Paul should take care of his arm. You know, for next year."

One coach smiled, the other one nodded his head.

"Reuven's right. Take the outfield," one of the coaches

said to Paul. "We'll just see how far Roy can go."

Reuven slipped back to his spot on the bench as Roy began his warm-up pitches. This was going to be trouble. Roy had made All-Stars because he was a great hitter. His pitching was only so-so, at best, and today he seemed really nervous. Every third pitch bounced in the dirt a foot or two in front of the plate.

Roy didn't improve much when the inning started. He struggled to put the ball over the plate, forcing Avi to scramble to keep balls from skipping by him. Reuven was more impressed with Avi than he wanted to admit. Avi had become a terrific catcher. He did exactly what a catcher was supposed to do. He used every part of his body to block wild pitches, getting hammered in the chest, the arm, and the shins. Even with the protective gear, Reuven knew that had to hurt.

One ball took a particularly bad carom and smacked Avi in the thigh—above the protector. He made the stop, anyway, and never said a word.

It seemed like Avi was limping a little after that. Reuven looked to see if either of the coaches noticed. They had been so worried about Paul's arm. Reuven wondered why they weren't worried about Avi's leg. Wouldn't it be a good idea for Avi to sit out an inning or two with an ice pack? Maybe, Avi should even sit out the whole rest of the game. After all, he got to be an All-Star. He didn't have to play every single inning, did he? If Reuven had been a real coach, he would have said something.

The real coaches didn't seem to notice anything, so Avi stayed in and continued to keep control of Roy's wild pitches. Thanks to Avi, the Blues got out of that inning only giving up two more runs. It was 6–4 Reds, going into the bottom of the fourth.

The first batter for the Blues walked. Avi came up next and, as always, swung at the first pitch. That boy would never learn. Avi didn't even have the swing sign. He was supposed to take the first pitch so the runner on first base could steal second. Imagine being an All-Star and not knowing enough to obey the coach's signs.

So Avi had swung at the first pitch when he wasn't supposed to and whacked the ball sharply between the first and second basemen. It skittered along the ground so fast that the right fielder couldn't stop it. The center fielder waited for it to ping-pong against the fence into his hands. By the time the Reds finally got that ball and heaved it back to the pitcher, the runner before Avi had scored and Avi was safe on first.

That was an RBI for Avi and a badly needed run for the Blues. So, instead of getting yelled at by the coach or maybe even being benched for not taking the sign, Avi was a hero.

"He lost his helmet," one of the coaches called to Reuven, pointing at Avi's helmet lying on the ground. "Do you mind getting it for him?"

The umpire signaled time, while Reuven jogged out with the helmet. If he couldn't be an All-Star himself, he might as well be a "run-and-fetch-it" for his kid brother.

"How bad's your leg?" Reuven asked.

"What? Oh that. It was nothing. I'm fine." Avi took the helmet. "Hey, tell the coach I'm sorry I swung. It was just right there, and I couldn't stop myself."

"Oh, sure. I'll tell him you're sorry you got an RBI."

Reuven trotted back to the bench, but he didn't bother to tell the coaches what Avi had said.

The next batter did take the sign. He held up on the first pitch giving Avi a chance to steal second. That batter struck out, and the next one hit a long pop-up to right field. Avi tagged up and made it easily to third base.

Two outs and the Blues were still down one run with Avi on third. Their next batter was one of the weakest on the team. He hit two fouls to quickly go 0 and 2. Then a third foul, followed by a fourth. He was making contact, but not getting any closer to fair territory. One more strike would end the inning with the Blues behind.

Avi danced off third base. He took one step—two steps—a third step. The pitcher spun and threw to Jack, who was playing third base for the Reds. Avi dove for the bag and was called safe. He brushed himself off, waited till the pitcher had the ball, then danced off the base again. One step—two steps—three steps. The pitcher spun and threw. Avi dove, once again arriving safely back on the bag.

The batter waited. The Reds' pitcher looked in for his sign. Avi danced. One step—two steps—three steps. The pitcher kept his eye on the batter. Four steps. The pitcher spun and threw. Avi dove and one finger—one single finger of his right hand—brushed the bag at the exact same instant that Jack brought the ball down against Avi's leg. Ties go to the runner, and the umpire flayed both arms out signaling that Avi was safe one more time.

Avi bounced up grinning. Reuven stared hard at his little brother. He could have sworn that Jack's tag was made on the same leg that Avi had bruised with that wild pitch. It seemed to him that it had been a hard tag. That just might slow Avi down a little, he thought.

The pitcher stared in, the batter waited, and Avi danced off the bag. Legs spread wide apart, he skipped sideways in broad hops. One step—two steps—three steps—four steps. The throw came a little too hard and a little too wild. Jack reached, leaned farther, sprawled across the slippery ground as the ball skipped by his outstretched fingers, and Avi sprinted for home.

The Blues' bench erupted in cheers, and they were still cheering when the batter struck out on the next pitch. At the end of the fourth, it was a tie game—thanks to Avi.

"That's base running, guys!" The head coach screamed, pounding Avi on the back. "That's determination. Make things happen, guys. You're supposed to be All-Stars here. That's the kind of aggressive play we need to have."

Avi just hunched over, strapping on his shin guards as if all the buzzing and cheering had nothing to do with him.

"What do you call that, anyway?" the coach went on.

"'Avi ball?' That's what I'd call that kind of playing. 'Avi ball.' I want to see everyone playing 'Avi ball.'"

Coaches. They sure can get carried away, Reuven thought.

The Blues suddenly got inspired, and they did play Avi ball for the next two innings. They were smooth in the field and aggressive at bat. But this was, after all, an All-Star game. The Reds weren't exactly going to sleep. By the end of sixth, the Blues were up 8–7, a lead of one lonely run.

Roy had pitched a good fifth inning, but he only survived the sixth inning with the help of excellent fielding. He had had it. There was no possibility of his pitching another inning. The Blues didn't have any other real pitchers, and the coach decided to use Avi for the last inning. Avi. As a closer. Imagine that. He held Avi out during the sixth inning to warm up with Reuven.

"Okay, Avi," the coach said. "Let's see if you can pitch as well as you catch and run bases."

"I'm not that great a pitcher, Coach. I only pitched a little during the season."

"Do your best. If you can hold them, we've won the game. If not, we still have another turn at bat."

Avi strode to the mound as if he had pitched all season.

"Avi luck" picked up where "Avi ball" had left off. The first Reds' batter caught Avi's first pitch for a towering blast right to the left fielder. Out one. The second batter ripped a grounder that could have been a double, but the shortstop made a really great play and got the out.

Avi had faced two batters, and he had two outs. One more and Avi would not only have been an All-Star, but he'd probably be the MVP of the game.

The next batter stepped in. Avi hit him with the first pitch. He didn't hit him hard, but there was definite contact. The batter took first base.

A tall, muscular kid took his place at the plate. Reuven recognized him. Howard "Something." He had played for the Mariners during the season and had gotten hits off Reuven twice, once for a double. He was one of the toughest batters that Reuven had faced. Maybe, just maybe, Avi luck was coming to an end.

Avi had been throwing solid strikes, with no speed and no action on the ball. These were just the pitches that good hitters loved, and this Howard "Something" was definitely a good hitter. He pulled Avi's first pitch far to the left for a foul. He fouled on the second pitch, too. Just barely. If it had stayed fair, it would have been an easy double or maybe even a triple.

Avi should have looked in to the catcher for a sign. Instead, he stared over at the bench, at Reuven. His next pitch was way outside for a ball, followed by one way high for another ball. He signaled for time, then bent down to tie his shoe.

Reuven had his small notebook tucked in his back pocket. In his mind, he could see the page listing Howard "Something" for the Mariners. He didn't even have to open it up. Reuven had studied that notebook so often, he had it memorized. Howard had very few weaknesses, and it had taken four or five at-bats before Reuven figured out what they were.

Avi was ready to make his pitch. He bounced that one in the dirt, sending a spray of damp dust into Howard "Something's" face and bringing the count full.

Good move, Avi, Reuven thought. Maybe if you blind him, he'll strike out.

Avi began manicuring the mound with his right foot. There must have been an invisible ruffle somewhere in that perfect-looking mound. Or was it that even Avi knew his luck was coming to an end?

Reuven watched his brother. When Avi had the mound perfectly groomed, he adjusted his belt and his cap.

Avi sure had turned into a heck of a catcher. If Reuven had wanted to make an entry in his book about Avi, he would have written: "great catcher, don't even try stealing on him."

He wished Avi had stopped him from trying to work on his curveball that Friday afternoon. Why couldn't Avi have just refused to help Reuven that day and gone into the house? He'd done that enough other times when he got mad at Reuven.

Avi seemed to have adjusted everything that could be adjusted and smoothed everything that could be smoothed. He stood there. On the mound. Frozen.

If Avi had just walked away that Friday afternoon, then

Reuven would be the one that was the All-Star. If Reuven had been an All-Star, he would have known just how to pitch this guy. If Reuven had never tried to learn the curve. If Avi had argued a little harder. If . . . if . . . if . . .

The umpire took a step toward Avi, so Avi leaned in and stared at his catcher.

Reuven hated this. He hated feeling jealous. He remembered the things the rabbi had said. About how being jealous wasn't really different from the coveting that you weren't supposed to do. And Reuven thought about Joseph—in the Torah—and all the bad things that happened because his brothers were jealous.

Reuven hated feeling jealous. He also hated watching his kid brother in an All-Star uniform.

Avi set for his pitch. He couldn't pitch well enough to get this guy out. Reuven knew that. And he could see in Avi's face that Avi knew it, too.

"Time!" Reuven yelled.

Both of the Blues' coaches leaned forward to look down the bench. The head coach nodded at Reuven, then turned toward the umpire with a shrug of his shoulders. Reuven was awfully glad now that he was wearing a coach's shirt.

"Sorry," Reuven mumbled to the umpire. "I need a time. Is that okay?"

"Sure, son." The umpire signaled a time-out while Reuven hurried out to the mound.

"This guy's really tough," he said when he was close

enough so that only Avi could hear him.

"I know. I know." Avi stared down at his foot as he gouged his toe into the perfectly sculpted mound. "Maybe I should walk him or something. I'm afraid if I throw anything decent, he'll hit it for a homer."

"Pitch him low."

"Low?"

"Yeah. Pitch him really low. It's the only garbage he swings at." Reuven patted his back pocket. "It's in my notebook."

"I guess I can try that."

Reuven started back toward the bench.

"Hey, thanks," Avi called to Reuven's back.

Reuven looked back, grinned, and flashed Avi a thumbs-up. Then he glanced over at the Reds' bench. Avi did, too. All the Reds were standing up, staring at them. "Just wanted to keep them guessing," Reuven said before he went to take his place back on the bench.

Avi swished his foot across the hole that he'd dug in the mound, then set for his pitch. The catcher sent a signal, and Avi shook him off. He shook off the next and the next. Finally, he nodded and made his pitch. It was low. Avi's pitch was so low, his catcher had to scramble to get in position for it.

Howard "Something" swung at that low ball like he was golfing, and still, the ball slipped by just beneath his bat.

Strike three.

In an instant, a swarm of blue jerseys buzzed the

mound. All of the Blues on the bench charged Avi, and all of the Blues in the field charged Avi. Even the coaches ran to the mound, pounding Avi on the back, hugging one another, and chanting—BLUES! BLUES! BLUES!

Reuven watched for a while from the bench, then began gathering equipment.

He looked up, his arms filled with bats, and saw Rachel Cohen standing nearby watching Avi and the Blues.

"That must be fun for Avi," she said quietly.

"Yeah. Guess so."

"It's too bad about what happened to your arm. You're so good, it seems like it should have been you really."

Reuven couldn't believe that anyone else could have been thinking exactly what he was thinking. And what she said should have embarrassed him, but her voice had been soft and her eyes had seemed a little sad. He didn't feel embarrassed at all.

"But I am happy for Avi. I didn't mean . . ."

"Yes. Me too," Reuven agreed. "Anyway, I'll do better next year."

"You will. I know you will." And Rachel turned on that bright, happy smile. "Hey, listen." She started to back towards her dad. "I'm in this musical this summer. Well, not exactly in it. But I play in the orchestra. Do you want to come? It should be really good."

"Sure." Reuven had never really thought much about musicals, but who knows? It could be fun. "Sure, I'd like to come."

Rachel headed off to join her family, but she took just enough time to look back at Reuven and wave.

Reuven finished stowing the equipment away before heading to the parking lot, too.

Avi was already in the car, and Reuven joined him to wait while Dad talked to the coach. Avi held that great shiny All-Star trophy in his hands.

"Thanks, Reuven."

"For what?"

"For helping me get that last guy out. I really thought I was going to lose the game for us."

"Hey, I was on the bench. You're the one that threw the pitch."

"But I wouldn't have known what to throw. That low pitch worked really well. You know, I don't think you would have done that. I think you would have just burned him with your fastball."

Reuven had no answer for that.

"I'm sorry about your arm, Reuven. I should have made you stop throwing that day when you hurt it."

"You tried, remember? I wanted to keep on."

Avi stared down at his trophy, turning it over in his hands.

"I'm still gonna learn the curve," Reuven said finally. "I talked to Dad last night. He said he'd help me this summer, a little at a time. He read in a book how to learn to throw curves, and the coach thought it would be okay if we didn't overdo it."

"It was fun, wasn't it?" Avi said. "When we had it working."

"Yeah. It was so great." Reuven dropped his voice almost to a whisper. "You've gotten to be a really great catcher, too."

"You think so? We work pretty good together, don't we? You pitching and me catching. We're a good battery. Just like Rachel Cohen said."

The boys stared out opposite windows at a sky that had become a jigsaw of glistening gold rays and hovering mist. A musky breeze moved through the car.

"Honor Roll's a pretty good thing, isn't it, Reuven?" Avi finally interrupted the quiet.

"Umm. I guess so. I would've rather made All-Stars."

"I mean. The thing is my grades aren't as good as yours. Do you think I could have any chance at Honor Roll next year?"

"I don't know. But anyway, if you have to write a term paper, I could help you come up with an interesting idea. I can give you some tips on what Mr. Graham likes, if you get him."

"Thanks." Avi grinned. "And, hey, next year, I can give you some tips on your pitching."

Just then, Dad arrived back at the car, which was too bad, because Reuven was this close to giving Avi a good pop in the arm. He would have deserved it.